SCARRED

THE BILLION HEIRS
BOOK 1

HELEN HARDT

VANESSA VALE

He's inherited billions, but he must leave his home and family to claim it.

She's no longer a captive, yet will she ever be free?

Austin Bridger is struggling to keep his seaplane business afloat and help his ailing mother. When his father, who never acknowledged his existence, dies, he leaves his billions to Austin and his two half brothers. The catch? To receive the inheritance, they must all live on his father's Montana ranch for a year. To Austin, the money's tainted, but because he desperately needs every dime, he has no choice but to leave Seattle.

Carly Vance was a student in veterinary school when her dream was shattered. Abducted from a diner in her small town, she was held captive on a South Pacific island for three years. Now she's home, but her scars run deep. Trying to reclaim her life, she bravely takes a job in Bridger Ranch's stables.

Despite Carly's painful past and Austin's responsibilities, sparks fly when they cross paths. But Bridger Ranch holds secrets—secrets that may threaten their happiness...and their lives.

a USTIN

"WHO'D YOU PISS OFF?"

I glance up at Ed, the dock guy helping me load the coolers of fresh oysters into the cargo area of the seaplane. My back is to the shore and I don't dare turn around. Not yet.

Ed looks down the length of the dock to someone I assume is heading our way. It's probably Cara—or Tara—from Saturday. After our night together, she somehow found out about my business—because we didn't do much talking—and has been calling around the clock. Showing up takes stalker to a new level because I am always straight with a woman. One night. A hell of a lot of fun, but no strings. All the orgasms she can take but nothing more.

"Fuck," I say under my breath. I take a second to close my eyes. Just what I need. Baggage besides the seafood I am about to shuttle to the resort up in the San Juans. "Redhead? Legs for miles?" I ask.

Ed's bushy eyebrows head north. "I wish. How about male, fifty and balding. I'd peg him as IRS except the guy's wearing a bolo tie."

I turn on the worn dock, the water lapping at the side. I catch a whiff of the briny tang of the outgoing tide. The man, who appears to be in his fifties, is headed our way and he's definitely not Cara. Or Tara. Ed's guess is pretty good, but as far as I know, the tax man is the one guy who doesn't have an issue with me.

"Mr. Bridger!" The man raises his hand as if to hail a cab. He wears a bolo tie along with a white shirt and crisp jeans. And he holds a square leather briefcase. Definitely a creditor.

Just what I need. I have enough issues dealing with the healthcare system on the phone about my mother's bills. In-person is a whole new level of pressure I don't want.

I set my hands on my hips and prepare for a battle. "If you want money, it'll only happen if I get these oysters in the air. They're not the paying customers you probably want to see, but they are alive. For now."

He stops in front of me and wipes his brow. For the Northwest, the weather is warm. Almost hot, even for summer. Another reason to get the plane in the air instead of lingering. Oysters and heat aren't a good combo.

He glances at the plane and then back to me. "I'm not here to take money from you, Mr. Bridger. I'm Tom Shankle, lawyer from Shankle, Smith, and Brazee."

Great. A lawyer. "I'm being sued." I turn my back on him, grab another cooler, and pass it to Ed. "Even better."

"You're not being sued."

With a quick glance, I see Shankle smile.

"You make visits to everyone who owes you money?" I stop mid-reach and stand upright. At six-two, I have five inches or more on the man. "If you bothered my mother with your money-grubbing shit—"

He holds up a hand. "I assure you I didn't bother her. She's not the reason for this visit. I hope her current treatments for multiple sclerosis are going well."

I frown. What's his angle?

"You know a lot about the health of a woman who's not the reason for your visit."

Mom's latest meds are part of a trial and aren't covered by insurance. Expensive. But working. She currently only has mild symptoms and I want it to stay that way, although she can no longer pilot trips for the business she founded. If Shankle wants to pull the plug on the treatment, that's a no-fucking-go.

Shankle rubs his jawline. "I've kept tabs on you."

Ed loads the last cooler and shuts the cargo door with a hearty slam that shakes the plane. He nods and ducks around the two of us as best he can for a guy his size. I can't blame him for steering clear of my shit, whatever the hell it is. Going to the back rope line, he waits for me to climb in and do my pre-flight checks. That's right, time to go. He'll help other planes that use this dock.

"Why the hell would you do that?" I growl, not liking anyone to *keep tabs on me.* Especially a lawyer.

"I've tried to reach you for the past three weeks." Shankle follows me to the front of the plane.

"Sorry, been busy running a business here. But you know that, since you're keeping those tabs and all." I climb onto the runner and reach to open the door, ready to get the hell out of here.

"I represent your father. Jonathan Bridger."

I freeze for a second and then turn, bobbing up and down along with the plane on the water.

"I'm not sure which is worse. Creditors or my fucking sperm donor," I grumble and glare. "Or a lawyer representing him."

"I assure you, I bear good news." Shankle offers a shaky smile.

"I don't give a shit about the man, just as he's never given one about me. Good news? The only good news you could bear is that he's dead."

He huffs out a laugh. "It seems I may have made your day then. He is, in fact, dead."

I blink, processing what he just said. "Holy shit." Then I grin.

The fucker married my mother and then divorced her before I was even born. Left her with nothing. Sure, he paid the obligatory child support, but that wasn't what she wanted from him. She expected love from a spouse. Not to be abandoned and for him to move on to another woman. Or two. Or fucking more for all I know.

My father was never a part of my life. Hell, I never even met him. Just hated his guts for what he did to my mom.

"How?" Yeah, I want to know what finally brought the man down.

"Brain aneurysm."

Instant and painless. Too bad.

"Thanks for letting me know." I open the cockpit door, ready to climb in and leave the bastard behind, just like always.

"There's more," Shankle adds.

I glance up at the sky. "That's enough for me. He's dead. Good riddance."

"I need fifteen minutes of your time."

"So do those oysters in the back." I point to the rear of the plane.

"Fine. I'll ride with you."

I glare again. Not what I expected. He steps down onto the runner behind me and opens the rear door, the one for passengers. The plane's small enough that it bobs from the shift in weight.

Lovering Seaplane usually takes passengers, but for supplemental income, we run supplies and various cargo. Like oysters. I'm used to customers, but not ones who climb aboard last-minute for a chat. In Shankle's case, it's to talk to me about my father, and most likely piss me off.

He can go along for the ride, but I don't have to make it easy on him.

I hold the door open as graciously as I possibly can. He tosses in his briefcase and awkwardly climbs up and into the back seat.

"Ever flown in a seaplane before?" I ask casually.

"Nothing smaller than the commuter jet from Missoula," he replies.

I smirk and glance at Ed, who shrugs. I climb into the pilot's seat and begin my pre-flight checklist.

"Mr. Bridger. Jonathan Bridger had a sizeable estate in Montana and—"

I hold up a hand to stop him. "I need to complete my checks, Shankle. In silence, unless you want me to miss something and risk us taking a two-thousand-foot swan dive into the Sound."

Shankle remains silent as I strap in and work through the list I have memorized, getting the engines on. I give Ed a thumbs up, and we're untied and airborne quickly, headed north. I adjust the yoke as we're buffeted by the high-level winds. Nothing too strong, but I don't fight them.

"As I was saying," Shankle shouts over the noise of the engines.

Out of the corner of my eye I see him trying to get his balance. I can barely hear him with my headset on so I tap my ear and glance back at him.

He grabs the headset in the back for passengers and puts it on. "Can you hear me now?"

His voice comes through all too clearly, annoying me, so I tip the yoke, dipping the right wing. The plane plunges a hundred feet or so and I pull up. When the guy reaches out to keep from flying across the cabin, I can't help a slight smile.

"Might want to strap in," I say. "Could get bumpy up here with choppy air and all."

It isn't all that rough. Low wind, clear visibility. A little bit of chop, just like the water below, but doable, if you're not prone to motion sickness.

His seatbelt clinks. "You have two half brothers."

My smile slips. I know about them. Both younger and from the women who took my mom's place. I turn the yoke again, dropping the right wing once more. Shankle gasps.

"The three of us aren't going to make a fort in the backyard and take blood oaths, Shankle. Get to the point."

I tap my sunglasses up my nose and straighten the plane. There is no autopilot, so I keep my gaze on the tree-covered rolling hills of the Pacific Northwest on the horizon.

"You and your brothers are heirs to his estate."

The man—our father—was rich. Obscenely so, and since I turned eighteen, I haven't seen a dime of it. Before then, I didn't get much. Enough for clothes and extra food. He moved on and so did my mom. She started the seaplane company from the ground—or in her case, the Puget Sound—up.

"Great. Mail the china and stamp collection to the company address. You didn't need to come all the way to Seattle." I don't raise my voice. I don't have to. I'm sure he can tell how much I hate my father through the headset loud and clear.

His laugh comes through just as clearly. "I assure you, Mr. Bridger, you'll receive more than a stamp collection. That's why I've been trying to reach you. Jonathan Bridger's fortune is estimated at over three billion dollars. You, along with your half brothers, Miles and Chance, are the sole inheritors."

The plane takes a nosedive. I'm not fucking with Shankle this time. I just can't believe what I'm hearing. The engine noise changes and my seat rattles.

"I'm a...what? A fucking billionaire?" I ask, righting the plane.

We're now a few hundred feet lower and Shankle's stomach is probably in his throat. Mine is too, for a completely different reason.

Money like that means no more oyster runs to ensure Mom's medicine is paid for this month. Mom can go to that specialist in Chile we read up on. Hell, she can buy *Chile*. No more creditors or business problems because she's sick. It means a second... or even a third seaplane. A freaking fleet of seaplanes. The charter business she started thirty years ago won't fold.

I go numb with sheer surprise of this information for only a moment. Piloting requires focus, and damn...this *is* good news.

I pull back on the yoke and aim for the stars. I can't

help a grin and a whoop of happiness. Dear old Dad can rot in hell while Mom gets well and flies again.

"I'll give you my bank account information when we land." I strum the yoke with my fingers, feeling fucking great for the first time in months. "You're right, Shankle. You do have good news."

Shankle is quiet, and I glance over my shoulder at him. He has his briefcase in his lap and a small stack of papers in his hands. "There is a catch."

I glance out the front window again and adjust course slightly. I've flown the area enough to recognize the sea and land below. Which island is which. There's no radar. No complex instrumentation.

"A catch," I echo.

Of course there is.

"You must return to Bridger Ranch in Montana."

Return? I've never been there. A few days away may impact flights. But if I have a billion dollars, what does it matter?

"I can swing a week off."

"You'll need a little more than a week." Shankle clears his throat. "The will clearly stipulates that all three Bridger sons must live and work at Bridger Ranch for the duration of one year to receive a dime."

"What the fuck?" I shout. "A year? I can't live in Montana for a year. My mother is sick and on special experimental drugs. If I don't get the money for a year, I can't stop working. The company will go under, and Mom—"

"It was your father's last wish."

"That I live in bumfuck Montana for a year? Give up my life, my business, risk my mother's health, all because some asshole is making me jump through hoops?"

As punishment, I dip the plane again, feel the pull against my harness.

Shankle whimpers.

A father who I never met and is dead—*dead*—is fucking with me and will continue to do so for an entire year. I have to go to Montana to get the money that will help my mother and save the company. But going will most likely make my mother's symptoms worse and will definitely hurt the business since I won't be able to fly.

"If it makes you feel any better, your brothers—"

"*Half* brothers."

"—aren't any happier. However, I *was* on land when I shared the news with them."

The cove where I will land appears in the distance. I adjust the flaps to begin our descent.

"We'll be on the ground soon, Shankle."

Really soon since I decide to come in hot. If I'm headed to Montana, I might as well have a little fun before

I'm grounded. And landlocked. And stuck with two men who share tainted blood.

"We're the billion heirs," I mutter.

Only a deadbeat—emphasis on *dead*—father would ruin it all.

 ARLY

ONE MONTH LATER...

THERE'S something soothing about grooming a horse. Something almost zen.

My father taught me how to do it when I was six years old. He wouldn't let me learn to ride until I could take care of the animal first. I hated him for it, of course. At that age, I didn't want to be bothered with such a mundane task. I wanted to be on horseback, riding wild and free, not brushing a horse's hair.

But that attitude didn't last. Grooming became a ritual for me—time getting to know the animal, time reflecting on our journey together.

Time contemplating something larger than myself.

It was my escape, and it's where I went in my head while I was held on the island.

My safe place.

"You're a gorgeous girl," I say to Ivory, a beautiful cremello quarter horse, as I grab the hoof pick. The tangy scents of the stable are familiar. Oddly comforting.

I've never seen a cremello before—not in real life, I mean. I saw all the colors in my equine textbook back in vet school. This mare has a creamy pale coat, pink skin, and blue eyes. Her mane and tale are a shade lighter than the rest of her. I run my hand down her flank, her hair soft and her body warm.

She's a gentle soul. One of my professors at school said blue-eyed horses were long thought to be wilder than their brown-eyed counterparts. As I work on Ivory, I can't help but wonder how that myth arose. Her temperament is more composed than any other horse I've known. I'm a stranger to her, yet she's giving me no trouble at all as I run my hand down her left foreleg.

"Up," I say softly.

Her ear twitches and she lifts her foot. Excellent. No

rocks. A little dirt, which I brush away with the pick. Her hoof looks healthy. She's been well cared for.

But of course she has. Her life is on the Bridger Ranch, where a veterinarian is on staff.

I'm merely an assistant. I didn't get to finish my first year of vet school...but I can't go there in my mind. Not on my first day at the ranch.

I have a job. A job working with animals I love. I smile to myself.

My first job since my return to Bayfield, Montana.

I gently place Ivory's hoof back on the stable floor and move to the next one, reliving the conversation with my parents this morning.

———

"I GOT A JOB. I START TODAY."

My mother's eyes go wide, and she continues pouring orange juice into my glass until—

"Mom, stop!"

She jerks the pitcher upright just before the glass overflows. "Sorry," she mumbles. "A job?"

"Yeah. At Bridger Ranch working in the stables."

"Bridger Ranch?" she repeats.

Dad's head whips up from the paper. He narrows his eyes

"With their livestock?" Mom asks.

I nod, feeling nervous and excited. "I'll help wherever they need me. Cattle, horses, dogs and cats. Chickens. I don't know. It's the first step to getting back to vet school."

"Why the hell would you get a job there of all places?" Dad's voice doesn't have his usual warmth. In fact, the way a vein throbs in his temple, he looks downright pissed.

"Because they have animals." The long list I just shared. Duh.

"Are you qualified?"

Classic Dad. He knows I'm qualified. This is about something else. Again, his words hurt.

"I've had almost a year of veterinary school and all the time I worked at the animal hospital in town during high school," I remind him.

"That was a long time ago, sweetheart," Mom says cautiously. She's worried for me, but all her sentiment does is remind me of what I missed out on. How far behind I am. What I lost.

Five years to be exact, but—

Dad slams his phone down on the table. "The answer is no. Fuck, no."

Mom gasps. "Rick. Watch your language."

"There are enough ranches in the area for you to work on. You don't have to work for the Bridgers."

I frown. "What's wrong with them? The head vet over at Bridger ranch thinks I can do the job as well as any vet tech."

I sigh, eyeing my father closely. I don't know what his deal is. It's one thing to worry about me and smother me by the day, but he's acting as if he doesn't like the Bridgers specifically. I thought they wanted me to return to my life. To be normal again.

"Besides, Dr. Lake thinks I'm ready. More importantly, I think I am."

God, am I. I need to get out of this house. I love my parents, but I'm twenty-seven years old, and they treat me like...

Well, like I could disappear at any moment...which I did five years ago.

Through no fault of my own, of course. At least that's what Dr. Lake has tried to convince me during the last year of therapy. I was in the wrong place at the wrong time—having lunch at Millie's Diner while home from vet school on spring break. Something as simple as that, in a small town in Montana, and my life changed forever.

I've only eaten at Millie's about a thousand times in my life, but why did I have to go that day?

That particular damned day...

No. Not going there. Not right now. I need to be whole today to begin this new venture.

Ernie, our golden retriever, swishes around my legs, yellow fur sticking to my jeans. I love this hound, but man, he can shed.

"Hey, Ernie." I ruffle his soft ears.

He's older now with a white muzzle. The years aged him, too. He smiles at me. Yeah, dogs can smile. I know they don't possess the requisite musculature, but I'm not convinced.

Ernie smiles. He doesn't care that I've got a job with the Bridgers.

And his panting smile always makes me grin—inside and out—even after the worst nightmares.

I've learned to live with them, and they're much less frequent than they used to be. I'm down to therapy only once a month now, and Dr. Lake says I'm ready to take the next step —a job—in returning to real life.

No, I have been living real life. Too real. But I have to look forward, not back.

Mom and Dad, on the other hand, aren't on board.

Especially Mom.

I get it. I do. She loves me, and she's fearful of losing me again. For those three years I was gone, they had to let me go. They had to believe I was gone forever and that I was never coming back.

They had a funeral, for God's sake...and then, three years later, Derek Wolfe was murdered and the other women and I were all rescued from that horrid island where we were held prisoners and hunted, tortured, violated by anyone who could pay to play.

Garnet, Moonstone, Tiger Eye, Opal, Amethyst, Sapphire... All of them.

And me.

Jade.

That's what I was called on the island because of my green eyes.

I swallow hard, pushing the memories back like Dr. Lake taught me. A wall built up brick-by-brick to surround the bad stuff. Not her words, but mine. The bad stuff.

"Carly," Mom says, "I'm not at all comfortable with this."

"That's right," Dad agrees. "Get a job, but I don't want my daughter working for that asshole."

Mom gasps again, sets her hand on her chest as if she has pearls to clutch.

I frown. "What's wrong with Chance Bridger?"

Dad stands, his chair scraping across the floor. "It's his father I hate. But like father, like son."

"What did Jonathan Bridger do?" *I ask.*

I remember seeing the older Bridger in town when I was young. I never spoke to him, but I don't remember Dad hating him either.

But I was gone for three years. Clearly something happened during that time, or earlier and I didn't notice. Was there a feud between the families before and I just wasn't paying attention? No. A lot changed recently. More than me. My dad is the mayor of Bayfield now.

Dad clenches his jaw and doesn't answer my question.

"You'd rather I remain bored here on our own ranch than get my life back?"

Mom ignores her words, clears her throat. "I agree, Rick. It's too soon. She's... She's not ready."

"Dr. Lake thinks I am." I stand so they see me and stop having a conversation as if I'm not even in the kitchen. If they don't believe me that this job is a good thing, they should at least believe her.

"We need to talk to Dr. Lake." Mom turns to the coffee maker and pours herself a cup. She won't drink it, though. She just needs something to do with her hands, which shake.

I feel for her. I do. I can't imagine what they went through. But I went through hell and I survived. I need this job. This... normalcy.

"I can't believe you don't believe me. I'm not lying."

Dad looks ready to punch a hole in the wall and Mom is gnawing on her lip, trying to hold back tears.

I push on. "I'm not a child, Mom. Dr. Lake is my therapist, and she can't talk to you without my permission."

"Then you'll give us your permission."

Seriously? I breathe in, count to ten. Mom is only trying to protect me. Dr. Lake and I have discussed it ad nauseum.

I'll never be whole again—at least not in the way I was before. But I can be happy. Happy and healthy and emotionally stable.

And productive.

I need to be productive. I need to get out of my parents' house and do something for myself.

"I want you away from that place. You want a job? Come work for me at City Hall. I've got leaflets about the ballot initiative to stuff into envelopes."

Stamp licking? Hell, no.

"I wanted to be a vet before. I want to be a vet now. This is a good place to start."

"Then work at the vet's office again. Or any other ranch in town," Dad counters.

I shake my head. "No. I'm not going to rescind now. It would be unprofessional, and besides, I want this job. It's a good one, one I'm excited about. The debate is over." I take a sip of my OJ. For the first time in a while, I put myself first. My parents are pissed, but they'll have to deal. "I start work today."

My dad storms out of the kitchen, the screen door slapping hard behind him.

———

I FINISH Ivory's feet and grab the round curry comb. Starting on her left side, I stroke her coat in a circular motion, keeping an eye out for any small injuries. As I move to her bony shoulder area, I lighten my touch to keep her comfortable.

She seems to be enjoying the attention. I'm not

surprised. Dad always told me that most horses enjoy a good grooming if it's done properly.

How I've missed this! Even the scents and strong smells of a stable. They're familiar and comforting.

Mom and Dad no longer keep horses on our small ranch. They sold the few they had when I disappeared in the effort to fund a search for me, so I haven't groomed a horse since...

I draw in a deep breath and inhale the sweet scent of straw and horsehair with only a tiny tinge of manure. These stables are kept clean. Really clean.

I haven't groomed a horse since...

It's okay to think the words, Dr. Lake says.

I haven't groomed a horse since before I was taken.

In reality, I mean. I groomed many horses in my mind while I was on that island.

I truly think it's what saved me. Thinking of the animals, all innocent and kind.

I reach Ivory's mane and encounter a small knot. "Sorry, girl." I disentangle the strands of hair. Once I'm done with the curry comb, I reach for the body brush to sweep away what little the comb loosened. The animal doesn't actually need a grooming, but the ranch's vet, Dr. Davis—she told me to call her Lexie, but it seems weird to call my boss by her first name—probably wanted to go easy on me on my first day. My past is well known in the area, unfortunately. I wish it weren't, but what can I do?

I see the looks, know people act differently toward me.

After the thorough brushing, Ivory snorts. I clean around her eyes and muzzle. "You're just gorgeous," I say to her again. "The most beautiful thing I've ever seen."

"I'd say the second-most beautiful."

 USTIN

THE WOMAN JERKS and drops the soft rag she was using on the horse. And damn, what a horse! I know planes, not horses, but that's got to be the most amazing animal I've ever laid eyes on.

And the woman? Even more incredible.

Fuck. Her long brown hair is pulled back in a high ponytail, and several strands have come loose. Her face has a sheen of perspiration, and she's wearing old jeans, a white T-shirt, and a pair of roughed-up cowboy boots, but none of that detracts from her smoking hot body, angelic face, and blazing green eyes.

Fuck, those eyes.

If she's what's been hiding in Montana, maybe I shouldn't have waited so long to visit my long-lost family.

She lifts her eyebrows and steps away from me. She raises her hands in front of her as if to stop me. "Who are you?"

"Austin Bridger. I—" I pause and take in the extent of the stables. One of the horse's stalls is probably half the size of my old apartment in Seattle...and it's air conditioned. A chuckle erupts from my throat. "Hell, I guess I own the damned place."

Or I *will*, after I spend the next year here with my brothers. Half brothers who I still haven't met.

"And you are...?" I continue.

She returns her gaze to the mare. "Carly. Carly Vance."

Her voice is soft and tentative, and it goes right to my dick.

"What are you doing here, Carly?" I ask, trying to prod information from her, even though it's obvious what she's doing.

Her tongue peeks out and wets her plump lower lip. "I work here. As of today."

She works here? Fuck it all. Screwing the help is never a good idea. I found that out six months ago when I had a few too many at a local bar and took my bookkeeper, Lori, to bed. Before we hit the sheets, I made it clear it was a casual, one-time thing, and she agreed.

Until the next day, when she demanded a raise or said she'd publicly accuse me of sexual harassment. Luckily, the female bartender overheard our conversation, so I had a witness. Once Lori realized she'd made a grave error, she quit. Good riddance. We couldn't afford a full-time book-keeper anyway. Mom's expenses were piling up.

So I'll look at Carly, but I sure as hell won't touch, no matter how much looking at her makes me consider otherwise.

I learned my lesson. Although my dick isn't in agreement.

Carly doesn't meet my gaze. Her stance is a little off. Is she...frightened of me?

I might be pissed about being in the state, being stuck with two half brothers I don't even know, hell, even life in general, but I would never hurt a woman.

"Did you... did you need something?" She darts her gaze up to mine and then away.

Yeah, I need to kiss those full pink lips. Get them wrapped around my—

I clear my throat and shift my stance.

"No. I'm just getting the feel of the place." The ranch is enormous. Shankle told me there are over fifty thousand acres. It'll take me most of the year to see all of it.

A frown causes her brow to wrinkle. "I thought you said you're the owner. Except...isn't Chance Bridger the owner since his father passed away?"

His father, *my* father. He's still dead. "Chance is my half brother."

Her eyes widen. "Oh. I didn't realize he had a brother."

"*Half* brother. And he has two, actually." I hold two fingers up.

Her eyes widen at the news. "There's another one?"

I nod and rub the back of my neck.

"Miles. We all have different moms."

"Oh." Pink rises to Carly's cheeks.

Which only makes her look more enticing.

My cock reacts. Again. *Down boy.*

"Well"—Carly clears her throat—"if there's nothing you need, I should get back to work."

Right. I'm her employer, after all, so I should make sure she's working. Except I'm not quite ready for our conversation to end because she's the prettiest thing I've seen since I arrived. Hell, I never saw anything like her back in Seattle.

There, I worked all the time to keep the business going. Took Mom to doctor's appointments when needed. Helped with chores around her house. I did everything *but* look for a woman.

Mom texted earlier, easing my mind a little.

· · ·

MOM: Greg's working out well. He's gotten the routes down and Ed tells me he doesn't suck. His words, not mine.

WE FOUND a fill-in pilot for me while I'm gone. The problem is that his paycheck eats into the overhead, so I don't know how long we'll stay afloat. Literally.

One year. One year and it'll all work out. Things will be tight for a little and then... no more worries.

Except Mom will still be sick.

ME: Good to hear. How's that new med working?

SHE ASSURED me she noticed a difference although I'm not sure if it's a lie because she's too stubborn to give an inch to her illness or because she doesn't want to add to my worries.

Either way, I can't do much to help Greg, the fill-in pilot, or Mom.

I refocus on the beauty in front of me. "What do you do here?"

"I'm a veterinary assistant." She doesn't move her gaze from the horse.

"Right. I heard we have vets on staff." For the fifty-plus

horses Shankle mentioned. Which I now own. Cows, too.

She lets out a cute little huff. "For an owner, you don't seem to know a lot about your own ranch."

I laugh and cross my arms over my chest. "Honey, I know *nothing* about this place. I just got here two days ago. I'm a city boy."

Her blush extends to her neck. "Honey? I'm not anyone's honey."

I raise my hands in mock surrender. "It's just a word, Carly. I call everyone honey."

She narrows her gorgeous eyes. "Do you call your brothers honey?"

I let out a guffaw. "Half brothers. And hell no. Just the ladies. If it makes you feel better, I'll try not to call you honey anymore."

She looks to the ground. "It's a very large ranch, Mr. Bridger. We may never see each other again, in which case you won't need to call me anything."

She's right about one thing. This ranch is fucking huge. But she's absolutely wrong about the other. I may not be able to take her to my bed, but I'm sure going to look to my heart's content. She sure is pretty. That long dark hair would look damned good spread across my pillow. The soft swells of her breasts are probably barely a handful, but I bet they're pert with perfect pink nipples. I wonder if I can make her come just from playing with them.

"It's Austin." I clear my throat. "And it would be a shame if I didn't see your pretty smile again."

Her cheeks take on a darker pink hue. I can't help but wonder if they match her—

"All right. Austin."

My whole body responds with a quiver when my name passes her lips. Fuck.

"We seem to find ourselves in a similar situation." I smile. "We're both new here."

"I don't find our situations similar at all," she retorts. "When's the last time you groomed a horse?"

I grin. "Around the fifteenth of never."

She shakes her head. "And you expect to run a ranch?"

No, I *don't* expect to run a ranch. I expect to fake it for a year so I can get my billion, and then I'll hightail it back to my real life in Seattle. The will might demand that I stay here and work the land with my half brothers, but I'm not sure how good I'll be.

"Is grooming horses a requirement to be a rancher?" I ask. If so, I'm going to have to learn. Hmm, I might have a good teacher in Carly. Maybe I could teach her a few things too.

She doesn't reply at first, and just when I think she's done talking to me—

"I grew up on a ranch, albeit a tiny one in comparison. It's just down the road. Horse grooming is one of the first things my father taught me." She frowns again, but this time I'm not sure why.

"I grew up learning how to fly," I tell her. "From my mom. Not the same thing at all."

A smile turns up the corner of her lips. "This ranch is big. I'm sure there's something you'll be good at, if not horses."

"I've got a year, so I'll have to find something to do," I grumble.

She frowns. "A year?"

I wave my hand. "Nothing."

Word of why I'm here and the rules behind it clearly hasn't spread to the staff, at least not to Carly. I've only met her and the housekeeper so far.

The horse whinnies and shifts her feet, distracting Carly. She runs her small hand down the animal's flank, and it's the first time I've ever been jealous of a horse.

"I'd better get back to work. I have another horse besides Ivory to groom." She glances my way and I can't miss the interest and curiosity. "See you around, Austin."

She grabs the lead and guides the horse down the center aisle of the stable. I watch the perfect sway of her ass in the snug jeans.

"Count on it, Carly. Count. On. It."

This year may suck, but at least I'll have a good view.

 ARLY

I'D SAY the second-most beautiful.

I can still hear the words in Austin Bridger's deep rich voice.

Austin Bridger...

Wow, is he good looking. Dark hair, dark eyes, a sculpted jawline, and that adorable dimple in his chin. And that body...my God.

There's a good reason I dropped the cloth I was using to wipe Ivory's face.

Attraction, pure and simple. In fact, attraction is too tame of a word.

More like captivation. It's startling, and so is he.

Once I turn away from him, I don't dare turn back until I hear him leave the stable. Then I let out a breath I only now realize I've been holding. My nipples are hard. And lower... I never thought I'd feel desire again. Or anything close to this. But now—

I lean against Ivory's soft body and breathe. Simply breathe.

Dr. Lake said I'd be interested in men again, but I didn't believe her. No way could I possibly. Not after what I've been through.

"It will catch you unaware," she said during a recent session. "I know you don't believe me, Carly, and that's okay. But it will happen. Those feelings are still inside you, and they will return."

"Soon?" I asked, trembling. I wanted to be normal, to feel like a woman. But it was difficult to trust even Dr. Lake. She hadn't been there.

"Probably not," she said, "but it will when you're ready. Did you get a vibrator like I suggested?"

I warmed at the question. She'd recommended I begin to take back my sexuality by getting a sex toy to use solo. To relearn my body and find pleasure in it. There aren't any adult stores around—if there were, I'd be too embarrassed to enter, anyway—so I ordered it online.

I nodded.

"Good."

She didn't ask what kind I'd gotten or if I'd used it or if I'd made myself come. I was thankful because just telling her I bought one was hard to share. So much harder than everything else I'd divulged. I'd bought one that had tons of five-star reviews, a fancy kind that not only vibrated against my g-spot inside but had a suction-like thing that went over my clit. It... God. I'd been embarrassed and fearful of using it, but the pull on my clit had been so intense it had wrung an orgasm from me before I could even think twice.

I'm trembling. I'm not sure how I kept from doing so in Austin's presence.

A vibrator is one thing. Austin Bridger is another.

When you're ready.

I'm so far from ready!

I let out a breath. I didn't tell Dr. Lake I was considering a one-night stand. A fling. A get-back-on-the-horse night of sex. Ripping off the proverbial Band-Aid. Whatever the term, I want to have it because I worry it will never happen. This feeling. Desire. Attraction. I don't want it to be me and my sex toy for the rest of my life.

But I *am* feeling. For Austin Bridger.

He doesn't know about my past.

He doesn't know anything about me.

A thrill shoots through me because all I saw was

interest in his gaze. Not pity or concern. Not fear of damaging the already broken Carly Vance.

My idea for a fling is growing. Maybe it's just what I need. A night with a man who doesn't know about my past. Who wants *me*. The complete version of me.

If he gives it to me, maybe I can be whole again.

I turn when someone enters the stable—a blond woman not much older than I am but who was able to complete veterinary school and nab the dream job as head veterinarian here on Bridger Ranch.

"Dr. Davis." I correct my stance. I've got to make a good impression on the boss. Lazing about lusting after the new ranch owner isn't the way to do that.

"Please, Carly. It's Lexie." She offers a kind smile and pats Ivory.

"Okay." I nod.

I'll try, anyway.

"How are you and Ivory doing?" She eyes the horse.

"Great. She's gentle, and my God, so beautiful."

"Isn't she?" Lexie gives Ivory another gentle pat on her flank. "I knew she'd be perfect for your first day. I didn't want to overwhelm you."

Of course. Everyone is tiptoeing around me as usual. I appreciated it at first, but now? It's getting on my last nerve. I'm fragile in some ways but not all.

"I want to work," I say, tipping my chin up. "I need to work, to be around animals."

"Well, we've got plenty of animals here," she says with a laugh. "But I'll need you to help with paperwork as well."

I nod. "Absolutely. Whatever you need."

"Blaine is on vacation for three more weeks."

I cock my head, trying to remember the name. "He's the other vet, right?"

"Yeah. A year out of vet school. This is his first vacation—some big family thing—and somehow it got scheduled the same week I had a vet tech leave because his wife got relocated, so I'm very glad you're here." She smiles.

It's a friendly smile. Lexie is pretty, in her blue-and-white western shirt and boot cut jeans, her hair in a low ponytail and a felt cowboy hat atop her head. She totally looks the cowgirl part.

"I'll brush down the other horse, but what else can I do for you today?" I ask.

"I'll get someone else to see to Maverick. I want to show you the kennels." Her eyes light up. "We've got a litter of pups that was born a week ago, and one of them is having trouble latching on. Would you like to feed him?"

"Of course. Let me put Ivory in her stall." I try to conceal my disappointment.

I love puppies, and bottle-feeding one sounds like

heaven, but I'm qualified to do so much more. How can I get Lexie to understand that?

I follow her out of the stables and toward a Jeep.

"Get in." She thumbs to the passenger seat.

A short drive later, we arrive at the kennels, near the main house.

The Bridger house.

I've seen it, of course, as it's on the edge of the property and visible when driving through the small town. It's made of local light stone. It's only one level, but because it's situated on some higher ground, everyone in town gets a good look at it.

And it's sprawling, meant for a huge family, not just the two men who have lived there until recently. Now I know it's three half brothers who share the space.

I'll probably never see the inside of it. This is as close as I've ever been, and it's spectacular. My family's ranch is a good size, even with the animals sold off, but it's nothing like this.

Austin Bridger lives there. In that huge house.

He sleeps there. In a bed.

God, a bed with Austin Bridger in it. All six feet plus of him. I wonder if he sleeps naked. I imagine that body beneath crisp white sheets. Like one of those calendars where he's Mr. February with the bedding barely covering his hips.

My nipples tighten.

Unbelievable. My libido has been dormant for so long that these feelings surprise me. I could do it. With Austin. If I can feel like this from just talking to him, my God... What would it be like if he touched me?

A touch of panic sets it. Would I freak out?

No. It's been long enough. I *want* to be with a man like Austin—a gorgeous man who's attracted to me. Who wants nothing more from me than pleasure because he doesn't know about my past.

I steady myself as I get out of the Jeep. I have one job here—to care for animals—but I can still lust after Austin Bridger. I could sleep with him, cross the first-time-since sex off the list, but I have a feeling I'd still be lusting. He'll just be *that* good. It'd be a step toward being myself again because I'm sure a guy as attractive as Austin would know what to do.

I follow Lexie toward the large building which houses the kennels. Barking sounds through the air.

"Chance breeds Australian Shepherds," Lexie says. "They're great with all the animals here. True working dogs."

"I'm sure," I say.

"Duchess is nesting with her pups in a separate area." Lexie bypasses the building and leads me to a smaller structure next to it. She opens the door. "Come on in."

A puppy nursery greets me. The puppies are so tiny, and they're snuggled against their mother, a gorgeous blue merle with one blue eye and one brown eye.

"Hey, Duchess," Lexie says in a soft voice. It's easy to tell how much she cares for the animals.

Duchess wags her tail.

"Carly, could you mix up the formula?" Lexie points to a canister on a counter and a jug of distilled water.

I nod. "Sure thing."

I read the directions on the formula and mix it into the small bottle.

Lexie brings me the tiny pup and I tuck him into the crook of my arm. He's a soft and warm little blob and I can't help but smile.

Lexie gives his tiny ear a small scratch. "He doesn't have a name yet, but do you see the slight deformity on his bottom lip?"

I nudge his lips apart gently. "Oh, yeah. Poor baby."

"He does much better with the bottle. It's best if you sit in that chair next to Duchess while you feed him. She doesn't like him to be too far away from her."

I take a seat and nudge the small nipple against his lips. He sucks eagerly at the formula.

"I'll check out Duchess and the other pups. Give them a once-over and make sure everything's good."

I nod, the small pup so warm in my arms.

He finishes the formula in record time, and I place him back against Duchess.

Once Lexie finishes with her exams, she turns to me. "I think you can call it a day."

I rise. "Okay. Are you sure? It's only"—I glance at my watch—"oh! It's five already."

"I know. Days fly by around here. I need to get home and shower, I'm going out tonight."

"Oh?" I glance at her left hand. No ring.

"Yeah, in fact..." She smiles. "Why don't you come along? It's ladies' night at the Dusty Rose."

God, the Dusty Rose.

I haven't been there since...

Think the words, Carly.

I haven't been there since before I was taken. Have they always had ladies' night? I never went in the past.

"What exactly is ladies' night?" I ask.

"Ladies get their first drink free and then half price after that," Lexie says. "I'm going with two girlfriends."

"What about...men?"

Will Austin be there?

"There will be men, of course. Ladies' night also brings in men." She bites her lip and casts her gaze down-ward. She remembers. "I'm sorry, Carly. I wasn't thinking."

The freaking elephant in the room rears its ugly head.

"No." I shake my head. "It's okay. In fact, I'd like to go."

The words come to me quickly. Too quickly because now I *have* to go. I *want* to go. It's time to...get laid. If I want to ask Austin to have sex with me, I need practice talking to men. Ladies night could help me make that happen.

"Good." Lexie smiles. "You can leave at any time if you're uncomfortable."

Funny thing is...I'm not uncomfortable. At least not at the thought. Once I get there, it may be a whole different story. The *idea* of having sex—consensual, fun sex—is a lot different than actually doing the deed.

I want to take my life back, and today—my first day at work—helped a lot. Why not go a little further? Besides, Lexie will be there, and while we're not friends—she's my boss—she is a familiar face.

This is all part of healing.

Of becoming Carly again.

Mom and Dad will *not* like this. If Dad lost his shit over me working here at the Bridger Ranch, he'll lose his shit at ladies' night.

Which makes it official. I'm going. I'm going to get laid. Soon.

"What time?" I ask.

"I can drive you. I'll swing by your parents' place at eight. That work?"

I smile. "I can't wait."

 USTIN

IT'S GOING to be a fucking nightmare of a year.

"Stuck with two city slickers." Chance, my youngest half brother, grumbles.

He drops his cowboy hat on an end table and goes to the bar—a full-fledged one probably salvaged from a vintage saloon—and grabs a bottle of beer, twists off the top and takes a big swig. He doesn't offer us one. Only gives Miles and me a cursory glance before swearing under his breath.

"Thank you for joining us," Shankle says, having popped to his feet when Chance stormed in. He's holding his briefcase just like in Seattle—as if it's glued to his hand. I wonder if he sleeps with the thing.

Miles just arrived from the airport, with Shankle as his chauffeur. I've spent two days here solo, bored out of my fucking mind. Besides the property being enormous, so is the house. And the stable. And the other outbuildings. Everything is big in Montana, it seems. The housekeeper told me Chance was in Livingston, wherever that is, at a horse auction, and Miles has only just been able to tear himself away from the Big Apple.

Miles leans against the back of a couch, arms crossed over his chest. He's relaxed, but watchful. Does he feel as out of place as I do?

He and I may have inherited part of this ranch, but this is Chance's home. He was raised here. He works the land. It's his job. His life. Now he's got two strangers he has to share it all with and a lawyer setting the rules from the will of a dead man.

A dead man none of us liked.

"I can't believe he's made you two come here. I mean, have either of you ever ridden a horse before?" Chance continues, ignoring Shankle. "Hell, do you know which end's for eating and which is for shitting?" He takes another deep swig.

For brothers, we look nothing alike. I have dark hair, Miles is fair, and Chance somehow came out a ginger. The only thing we all have in common with our father is size. We're all over six feet. Miles is the tallest. Chance is barrel-chested and has about twenty pounds of extra muscle, probably from tossing hay bales all day.

It's not just our looks. Our dress is different too. Chance is clearly a rancher with his sturdy work boots, big cowboy hat and snap shirt. His hair's short and tidy, his face cleanly shaven. Miles is in dark jeans, motorcycle boots and a black T-shirt with a week's worth of scruff on his cheeks.

"I'm sure they'll learn some valuable skills while here over the next year," Shankle offers, clearly trying to be diplomatic.

"I met a pretty new vet assistant who can help me out," I reply, thinking of Carly and how she knew her way around a horse. She was skittish, but I couldn't miss the way she raked her gaze over my body. There was interest there—mutual interest—that might make the time here fun.

"Who?" Chance narrows his eyes.

"Little thing with dark hair. Said her name's Carly."

"Not Carly Vance."

I raise my eyebrows. "Yeah, Carly Vance."

"Leave that one be." He shoots me a look that would wither the balls off a weaker man. "Head into town to the Dusty Rose and pick up a willing cowgirl. Any woman in town—single or otherwise—learns your last name is Bridger and you'll have more pussy than you can handle."

If Chance thinks he's steering me away, he's dead wrong. "Is Carly taken? She yours?"

I don't poach, but I also don't want to get shot either. If she is Chance's woman, she's out of play. I don't blame him for his protective stance. If she were mine, I'd shoot first and ask questions later if a guy came sniffing around.

"Taken? You could say that." He sets his beer down with a clatter. "She's off limits. For both of you."

Taken by whom? If she's not Chance's, whose is she?

Chance darts his gaze between us. "Hell, I've got two brothers and I don't even know who's who."

"Austin," I say.

"Miles." He doesn't look fazed by Chance's anger. Maybe it's the New Yorker in him, or maybe he's just chill. He holds up his hands. "As for this Carly woman, I don't even know who you're talking about, but it's nice to know there's pretty *scenery*."

Miles is clearly single.

"I understand you don't want us here, Chance, but this wasn't our first choice either." He looks to me. "I assume I can speak for you and say we have lives that *aren't* here."

I nod. "Pull out your dick and pee on everything," I tell Chance. "It's all yours."

Miles laughs, and Shankle looks—well, a little horrified.

"You can keep the house and the furniture," Miles continues. "Even the horses. The only thing I like to ride —besides a pretty woman or two—is a motorcycle. But I earned my third."

"Earned?" Chance shakes his head and lifts his gaze to the ceiling. The really high vaulted ceiling. "You didn't earn shit, either one of you. I'm the one who's worked this land all my fucking life. I knew you two existed, but he never talked about you. Neither of you. Not once."

He turns his blue gaze my way. It's ice-cold and full of anger—anger I recognize.

I can relate to his frustration. I don't want to be here any more than he wants two strangers invading his space. And taking a share.

Still, I bristle at the fact that my—*our*—father cut us so completely from his life.

"Mention?" I say. "I never *met* the asshole. He ditched my mother when she was pregnant."

Miles nods. "Same. Seems like Daddy didn't like to wear a condom or commit to wives or kids."

"Gentlemen, I think—" Shankle begins.

Chance cuts him off, waving his beer in the air. "You think I liked the man?" He curls his lip and takes a big swig. "He kept my mother around for a few years and then divorced her ass, too. She's living it up in Boca Raton. Now the two of you are living it up here."

Seriously? What a fucking dickhead.

I shake my head. "Living it up? I'm a fucking sea pilot with bills to pay. I might be a billionaire, but I'm pretty fucking poor for another fifty weeks or so."

"That's true," Shankle says. "The will stipulates the entire estate will be held in trust until one year after your father's death. If you remain at Bridger Ranch for that duration, it will be split evenly between the three of you."

I frown, though this part isn't news to us.

"We can't leave at all?" From Miles.

"Why would you need to leave?" Shankle asks.

"Because we have lives," Miles says.

A throat clear from Shankle. "There are stipulations."

Miles rolls his eyes but he doesn't ask for elaboration. Neither do I. What good will it do?

Shankle continues, "You may not draw on the money prior to that date, although while you live here and learn about the ranch—"

"Excuse me," Miles cuts in. "*Learn* about the ranch?"

Shankle clears his throat. "Well...yes. Your father specifically states in the will that he wants the three of you to run the ranch together."

I rake my fingers through my hair. "For Christ's sake."

"You'll get an allowance," Shankle continues, "and of course your room and board will be provided."

"Where?" Miles asks.

"Here, at the main house. The three of you will live together."

"In bunk beds, Daddy?" Miles jokes. "And if we fight, we won't get our allowance, right?"

I chuckle. Chance may be a huge dick, but Miles? He's growing on me. We may have grown up on different sides of the country, but we're stuck here in the middle now.

"The house is big enough for you each to have a private bedroom and bathroom," Shankle says, completely ignoring Miles's sarcasm. "Austin already knows this, since he's been here for a few days."

"How much is this allowance?" I do some mental calculations on how to keep the business afloat and bills paid.

"A thousand dollars a month," he says. "But remember, you're not paying for food or shelter."

Right. For billionaires, we aren't even breaking the poverty line.

"Here on the ranch," I say, thinking of the mortgage on Mom's house. I moved all my things into a storage unit and canceled the lease on my place, but there are still bills.

Miles laughs. "Yeah. I'm sure as shit paying for *shelter* in New York."

A thousand dollars a month. I actually make more piloting a seaplane.

My life in a nutshell—

The woman who makes my dick throb is taken.

My mother is ill and alone back in Seattle.

My littlest brother already hates me.

And I'm the poorest fucking billionaire on the planet.

Great. Just great.

All Chance has to do is keep right on living his life, foaling calves or mending fences or whatever he does around here to get his billion. Miles and I have to uproot our whole lives.

Chance finishes his beer. This time, when he goes to the fridge, he grabs three by the long necks. He turns and tosses one to me and the other to Miles.

I consider it an olive branch as I catch it. "Thanks."

"Tell us, Shankle, the one thing I'm sure all three of us are wondering," Chance says. "Why?"

"Why?" Shankle repeats.

Chance nods. "Yeah, why? Why would my old man leave his fortune to kids he doesn't care about? Sure, they're his blood, but why give them something now when he didn't give them shit before?"

It's a great question, one I've wanted the answer to since Shankle climbed on my plane.

"Well, I can't—"

"And why force them to stay here? It does no one any fucking good. Austin has seaplanes to fly. And Miles... well, whatever the fuck he does, I'm sure it's not here either."

"I do custom builds. Motorcycles and cars. A fancy mechanic." Miles pulls out a stool at the bar and sits. "I'm curious, as well. Why would Daddy dearest do this to us?"

I nod. "I'm interested to know, too."

We look to Shankle.

"I don't know the answer," he says, scratching his head. "It's my job to ensure the will is legal and holds. I had no say in what Jonathan put in it."

Chance frowns. "You're no fucking help."

"I have no intention of getting in your way," Miles says to Chance. "I might be able to repair your tractors and ATVs, but I'll happily steer clear of the stables and...all of it."

"I'm going to be pretty bored unless you've got a plane," I add.

Chance laughs. "Oh, we've got a plane. Or two. Since you fly seaplanes, you might need some training wheels."

"I can fly whatever you put in front of me," I reply.

Shankle makes a funny choking sound, but I ignore him.

For the first time all week—other than when I stumbled across Carly earlier—I feel excitement. Man, I'd love to get back up in the air.

"Can you use a hammer?" Chance asks.

I nod, trying not to be insulted.

"Breakfast's at six," he says. "We'll head out after that."

"Doing what?" I ask.

"Got about twenty miles of fencing to check and fix." He grabs his hat and his beer bottle.

I look to Miles and then to Shankle.

"I am only here to ensure the three of you follow the letter of the will," Shankle tells us. "You're off to a good start."

"It's going to be a long year, brother," Miles says to me. "Something tells me it's going to be a wild ride."

"Wild is good," I say. "Better than boring like the past two days. The will doesn't say we're stuck on the ranch, right, Shankle?"

He shakes his head.

I look to Miles. "Why don't you and I check out this Dusty Rose place later?"

"Are you fucking serious?" Chance's voice is laced with surprise. "Did I not just say breakfast is at six?"

Miles looks at me, amusement tipping up the corner

of his mouth. "I think that's what he said. But maybe there's a problem with my hearing?"

"Nope," I tell him. "That's what he said."

"Still want to go?" Miles grins.

"Hell, yeah."

Chance scoffs. "You're going to make plans without me? What the fuck kind of brothers are you?"

"Dude," Miles says, "you can't even look at us."

"Maybe not"—Chance takes a swig of his beer—"but I can sure look at the fillies over at the Dusty Rose. It might even be ladies' night."

"Ladies' night?" I lift my eyebrows. "Sounds like the perfect time for our first brotherly outing."

"I THINK I LIKE LADIES' night," I say with a grin.

Lexie and her friend Amanda laugh. Apparently their other friend Gracie bailed because her mom had issues with her dishwasher.

"It's the Long Island Iced Tea talking." Amanda points to my mostly empty glass. "Free drinks and eye candy everywhere you look."

I glance around, agreeing. Ladies' night may bring in the women, but there isn't a shortage of men. They fill the bar and I'm enjoying the scenery. I'm not used to the crowd or the noise level, but it's so...*normal* in here. Easy to relax. No doubt the drink helps.

I've been back in town a year and I haven't done anything like this. It makes me realize how boring I've been. How sheltered. How...scared.

No one here has the same not-normal experience as I do. No one here has been taken. Lost three years to...

No!

My thoughts need to stay on the snug Wranglers and chiseled jaws.

"Alan hates when I come to these things." Amanda waggles her eyebrows as a very attractive cowboy walks up.

He tips his hat to us and grins. "Buy you ladies a drink?"

My tongue is a knot in my mouth. Before... I only casually dated and rarely went to bars. I was barely twenty-two when...

Stop it!

"Drinks are free, cowboy," Lexie says, her smile softening the blow.

"I can offer you other things," he adds with a wink.

I warm, surprised by his boldness.

"It's a girls' night," Lexie replies, "but if we change our minds, we'll wave you down."

He gives us a tip of his hat and he's off.

He didn't push. Didn't get angry. He's a decent guy.

"God, Alan would lose his mind if he knew someone tried to pick us up," Amanda says, taking a sip of her drink.

"Makes Alan appreciate what he's got in a fiancée," Lexie reminds her. "You can look, but not touch. Me? I may want to touch. I'm keeping that guy on standby."

Amanda laughs and I do, too. Since Lexie is the designated driver, she's drinking a soda while Amanda and I are enjoying the free and discounted alcohol.

Lexie picked me up right at eight as she promised, and then we went to get Amanda from her house in town. After the blowup with my parents this morning, they were remarkably quiet about me going out. They never commented before I was taken and today it seems they're picking their battles. Going out with two other women to ladies' night at a bar is more acceptable than a job. Go figure.

"I might want to touch too," I say softly.

They whip their gazes to mine.

I warm under their surprise. "What? I can't pick up a guy?"

Amanda claps her hands and squeals, making heads turn in her direction. She's pretty with chin length blond hair and blue eyes. She told me in the car she was a nurse at the local pediatrician's office and that she was getting married in the fall.

"You can," she says. "You *so* can."

Lexie sets her hand on mine. "You're sure?"

"Because of what happened?" My voice is soft. That liquid courage is evaporating like a creek in the summer heat.

She shakes her head, her hair sliding over her shoulders. "No, because you're gorgeous and amazing and whoever you pick's going to turn into your slave."

The word makes me blanch and my stomach sour.

"Shit." Lexie grabs my hand and gives it a squeeze. "That was thoughtless of me to say."

"It's true," Amanda says. "You're so pretty. I'd kill for your thick hair. And your curves. I can't fill a B cup if I stuff it with toilet paper."

She's tall and willowy and confident. She's attractive, but it's the way she's content in being herself that has me envious. She doesn't second guess everything like I do.

She clearly doesn't know what happened to me. This is a small town and everyone knows everything about everybody else. Or so I thought. Maybe what happened to me isn't that big of a deal to anyone else.

And it shouldn't be.

Maybe I've been with my parents too much since my return. They've been so protective, *overbearing,* and while I understand their feelings, I have to break free if I'm going to truly heal.

This is good, coming here. A word can't set me off. I can't let it.

I climb off my stool. "I'm going to run to the ladies' room."

Lexie snags my wrist. "I'm so sorry."

Because I was held captive on Derek Wolfe's island for three years? Lexie knows about what happened, at least that I was taken and finally set free, but not the details. It's easy for anyone to make a mental leap as to what I endured.

"It's fine," I reply. "The drink went right through me. I might be ready to...to—"

"Get laid," Amanda says for me.

I smile, thankful for the loud music so no one hears her. "Yeah, I might be ready to get laid, but picking a guy makes me a little nervous."

A new song comes over the hidden speakers and everyone hoots and hollers, apparently happy with the choice.

"Understandable," Lexie replies over the noise.

"Maybe I should go with the guy who offered to get us drinks...and other things." I nod to Lexie. "Or did you want him?"

"You can have him. But why limit yourself?" she says,

waving her hand around. "When you come back, we'll scope out the options. If you're going to go home with a guy, we'll make sure he's a good one."

Amanda nods.

I swallow. Maybe I should have kept my mouth shut. While the men in the bar are attractive, for some reason only Austin Bridger makes me come alive. I felt something just looking at him in the stable earlier. Talking to him, too, although I didn't like being called honey. I don't like pet names. I had many on the island—including my gem name, Jade. From now on I just want to be Carly.

The line moves quickly and I'm out of the bathroom faster than I want. I walk out, head down, as I shake my hands dry—the paper towels are all out—and—

"Oh!"

I collide with someone—someone solid. And tall.

I step back and apologize to a broad chest. Then I look up.

"Hello, Carly."

Oh God. I suppress a quiver.

Austin Bridger. Austin Bridger, who's even better looking than I remember.

Did I conjure him from thin air? Or is it just luck?

Or maybe bad luck because now Lexie and Amanda know I want a fling and Austin's here and I'll have to tell them about him and—

He sets his hand on my arm. "Take a breath. I'm not that scary."

Take a breath? Am I...

God, yes, I am. My breath is coming out in small puffs.

And no, he's not scary. Not scary at all. I *know* scary all too well.

"Sorry." I roll my eyes. My heart rate slowly settles. "Hi."

He smiles.

And I melt. So do my panties. That grin should be illegal.

"Hi."

"What are you doing here?" I ask.

His hand is still on me and he pulls me to the side as a woman comes down the hall. He settles himself so I'm shielded by anyone else who might come by.

"I'm here with my brothers."

"You mean your *half* brothers?"

He shrugs his broad shoulders. "We're getting to know each other over beers"—his intense gaze dips from my eyes to my lips—"and pretty women."

"I'm here with Lexie, one of your ranch vets, and a friend of hers."

"I'll walk you back then."

He slides his hand down my arm to interlock his fingers with mine. Yes, we're holding hands, and it feels...

Nice. Too nice.

I glance at him as he works his way through the bar. People clear a path to let us through. With my free hand, I point to the high-top where Lexie and Amanda are talking with their heads close together.

When I slide onto my stool, they stare up at Austin, and then down at our joined hands.

"Looks like you don't need our help," Amanda says to me with a sly smile. "I'm Amanda. That's Lexie."

"Austin."

He's not in full cowboy-wear. He does have on jeans and they do amazing things with his sturdy thighs, butt, and... package. I take in his black T-shirt, how it showcases his muscles beneath. Finally, I look at his face.

He winks.

Shit. I'm caught ogling and my cheeks heat.

"I'm new to town," he says. "Carly's one of the only people I know."

"Where are you from?" Amanda asks.

"Seattle."

"You in town long?" This time the question comes from Lexie.

"A year."

"He's your new boss," I tell her.

Lexie frowns, clearly confused.

"I'm Austin Bridger."

Her eyes widen. "Ohhh..."

"So you're not sticking around," Amanda states. "After the year."

"No."

"Single?" From Lexie.

"Yes."

"Gay?"

"No." His lips twitch. "I'm the boss, why do I feel like I'm being interviewed?"

Lexie and Amanda look my way and shrug.

A blond man sidles up to stand beside Austin. "I thought you were bringing us beers."

Austin's half brother I bet. Another man moves to flank his other side. This one I know. Chance Bridger.

"I got distracted." Austin's hand slips from mine. "This is Amanda, Lexie, and—"

"Carly." Chance pulls me in for a hug and then lets me go as if I were made of burning lava. "Sorry."

He runs a hand over his red hair.

His reaction is just what I hate from people. Fear. Of touching me. Hurting me. Saying the wrong thing.

Austin and the other brother wrinkle their foreheads at his overreaction.

"Hey, boss," Lexie says. "Although I guess that refers to all three of you, if you're the other brother." She looks to the blond.

He smiles. And wow, he's handsome too with his fair hair and pale eyes. The three Bridger brothers look nothing alike, but they're all astonishingly handsome in their own way.

"Miles. And yes, I'm the *other* brother." He has bad boy written all over him.

"Didn't know there were *three* of you Bridger boys," Amanda says. "Might make ladies' night pretty easy. Why don't you join us?"

They move to track down stools and I lean in and hiss in her ear. "What are you doing?"

Lexie leans in, too. "You want a one-night stand, those men are perfect options."

Amanda nods eagerly.

"Take your pick," Lexie continues. "Do you like dark, fair, or redhead? You couldn't ask for a better selection."

Amanda giggles. "She's right. I'm not sure which one I'd choose. I'd have to take a little of each." She moans and I frown. "Or all three. At the same time. Can you imagine?"

"You need to go home to Alan and role play or something," Lexie snarks.

"I can imagine, but no." Amanda grins. "They're for Carly."

"What's for Carly?" Austin settles his stool directly

beside me. He sits and his face is inches from mine, our shoulders bumping.

This close, I can see the gold flecks in his dark eyes. The five o'clock shadow on his square jaw. I can breathe in the scent of him—soap and dark woods.

Lexie and Amanda shift so Miles is between them, snugly because of his broad shoulders. Chance ends up on my other side. They set their beers on the table.

"A man."

Lexie's words bring fierce warmth once again to my face. Thank God for the dim lighting. I'm sure I'm red as a tomato.

The men swivel their gazes to me and I want the floor to swallow me up. I'm not as brazen as my new boss.

"A man?" Chance's voice is deep and rough.

As he says it, I feel Austin's body go taut against mine.

Ladies' night is one thing. Being offered drinks by handsome men is another. So is telling two new friends that I'm ready to have sex. To use a guy to get over my hang-ups. But telling three handsome brothers who are signing my paycheck?

I hop to my feet as best I can wedged between two big men, grab my clutch, and bolt.

It's not as easy to cut through the crowd as Austin made it seem. I finally get to the front door and push it open, taking big gulps of cooler air. I cut around the side of the building, lean against the hard brick.

"Carly!"

I stiffen at the shout of my name.

A few seconds later, Austin appears around the corner.

It's dark and he's cast in a blue glow from the neon bar sign.

"Are you okay?"

I look at the front of his T-shirt and nod. "I overreacted. I should have laughed it off because Lexie was having some fun and helping me and I'm not used to—"

"What man is she talking about? Who? Are you afraid of him?" He looks around, but we're alone. "Do I need to go beat someone up?"

I smile and shake my head. God, he's protective. "That's really sweet of you."

He sets a hand on the wall above my head and leans in. "Me? Sweet?"

He's right. He's not all that sweet. But do I want sweet? After what I went through, flowers and candlelight, soft music, and a plush bed should be what I want. But meeting Austin—even barely—has changed my thinking.

He's rugged and rough and he probably touches a woman the same way. Protective, but at the same time, possessive.

"What's going on?"

I close my eyes for a second and take a deep breath.

This is it, an opportunity to reclaim a piece of myself. I can tell him the truth, that I want to have sex with him. Or I can slink away like the broken, fragile snowflake everyone treats with kid gloves.

"Carly…"

I don't tell him because I won't be able to get the words out. *I want to sleep with you. Please have sex with me.*

As if. I don't scurry off. Instead—

I rise onto my tiptoes and kiss him.

For a moment, he doesn't do anything.

What am I thinking? This is a mistake. Of course he doesn't want me. Broken Carly. Shy, defective, crazy Carly. Until—

His arm bands around my back, his other hand cupping the back of my head, and he takes over.

Thank God.

His lips meld to mine, and he's angling my head to take the kiss deeper. His lips are soft, but the kiss is potent, full of need. I whimper at the deliciousness of it.

I'm being kissed!

His tongue finds mine. He tastes of beer and man. His hardness presses me into the building.

"Carly," he whispers as he kisses along my jaw.

I stare up at the pitch-black sky. He's aggressive with

his hands, moving to cup my ass and my breast. His touch is gentle, but insistent.

I love it. Need it. My nipple hardens beneath his fingers and my panties are no doubt already damp. If he touches me there, he'll know how much I desire him, how much I need this.

I'm not broken. I'm not frozen. With every kiss, nibble, and lick, with every squeeze and caress, I'm melting. Softening. Heating.

Healing.

"More," I whisper, rocking my hips into his. I can feel the hard length of him and he's not small. Anywhere.

"Fuck, you're perfect." He moves his hand from my butt to cup me over my jeans.

I moan and then bite my lip. God, did that sound come from me?

I feel a smile pull at his lips as they move along my neck. "Like that?"

I roll my hips so he'll press harder. The friction feels *so* good.

"You want to come, sweetheart?" His words are rough, spoken close to my ear. I should hate the endearment, but he's cupping my center.

Do I want to come?

Yes. I do. I *so* do. My vibrator makes me come, but it

doesn't make me feel like this. Hot, needy. Achy. Desperate.

I nod. "Yes. Please."

He deftly slides down the zipper to my jeans, and then he slips his hand into the gap and beneath the simple cotton of my panties.

He slides his fingers over me...and then into me. I gasp.

"You're soaked," he breathes against my neck. "Is that all for me?"

I can't do anything but nod and let my head fall back against the wall. I haven't been wet for a guy in forever. I'd be embarrassed how I respond to him, but he's... God, he's touching me just how I need. He's skilled, his fingers curling inside me with expert precision indicating that he's far more experienced than I am.

Yet I'm glad for it because it feels so good. We're standing, fully dressed, outside a bar. If it's this good here...

Holy shit.

I grip his wrist, not to push him away, but to hold on. I feel his tendons work as he rubs my clit and pushes me close to the edge. His mouth is on my neck, and he's licking and sucking, surely leaving a mark for me to find tomorrow.

"Austin, I'm going to—"

"What the fuck is going on here?"

The shout breaks through the fog that is now my mind. Austin's lips are instantly gone. So is his hand.

I'm so aroused I want to cry, but the voice is like an ice bath. Austin shifts to block me, and I can't see who's interrupted us.

"Is that *Carly*?"

"Chance, leave us the fuck alone," Austin says.

Oh God, it's Chance Bridger. I fumble with my jeans, working the zipper back up.

"I told you to leave her the fuck alone," Chance snarls.

They talked about me?

"I'm a grown man and you will *not* tell me what to do. Do not shame Carly like this."

"Shame her? I'm not the one who had his tongue down her throat and his hand in her pants."

I move to step around Austin, to tell Chance I'm the one who kissed Austin, that I wanted what he was doing.

For the first time in over five years, a man touched me because *I* wanted it. He was *giving* me pleasure. I'm not ashamed by my actions with Austin. Only by Chance calling us out as if I'm a teenage girl who doesn't know her own mind.

Austin is right. I do feel shame.

Before I can say anything, my body still humming with awakened need, Chance's arm rockets out and punches Austin in the face.

 USTIN

A DULL THUD.

Not the pop you hear in the movies.

It's been a while since I've taken a punch—I gave up bar brawling years ago—and I forgot.

A hard fucking strike, and my head almost hits the brick of the building.

"Chance, no!" Carly's voice.

I rub my jaw. My little brother—*half* brother, the dick-weed—has nice form, but didn't put enough power behind it to even think about taking me out. Surprising, really. The man looks like a tank. Plus, if I'm dead, he gets more money.

"I'm taking you home, Carly." Chance takes Carly's hand.

Jealousy erupts in my gut.

Without thinking, I grab Carly's arm and yank her out of his hold. "Like hell you are."

"Austin," Chance says, "I told you she was off limits."

"Off limits?" Carly shrugs me off crosses her arms. Her glare is directed at Chance. "And just who are you, Chance Bridger, to decide I'm off limits?"

"Carly…" Chance shakes his head.

"The lady doesn't want to go with you." I take her hand once more, this time more gently.

"Austin, you don't know—"

Carly rips her hand out of mine once more. "Shut up, Chance. Just shut up." She scans the small crowd that has gathered. "The same goes for all of you. I'm so tired of being everyone's pity case. I'm so freaking tired of all of it!" She races around the building.

Pity case? What's she talking about? I attempt to follow her, but Chance grabs my arm and holds me back.

"I swear to God," I grit out. "We may share a father, but I will fucking take you out, man."

He scoffs. "I'd like to see you try. I was holding back before."

Turning, he waves off the onlookers. "Show's over."

They don't move.

"I said get the fuck out of here!" Chance yells.

They disperse and only Chance, Lexie, and Amanda remain, the rustling of the wind through the nearby pines and crickets chirping fill the air.

"You may be the size of Mount Rainier, but I grew up dodging the drug gangs in Beacon Hill, and I've been in a few bar fights in my day, which I'm betting you haven't," I tell him. "I can take you easy."

"Just stop it, both of you," a blond woman—Lexie, if I recall correctly—says.

Right. Lexie. In fact, she works for Chance. *Us.* A vet.

"Stay out of this, Lex," Chance says.

"No." She steps close. "You can fire me if you want to, Chance, but I'm going to say something here. I realized something today as I watched Carly work. I went easy on her, it being her first day and all. Let her feed the puppies. I was wrong to do that. Dead wrong."

"What the fuck is she talking about?" I demand. "What's wrong with Carly?"

I can't think of a single thing.

"That's just it," Lexie continues. "There's *nothing* wrong with Carly. She's a lovely young woman who's had some bad luck. Really bad luck. But she's healing, and—"

Healing? Jesus, she's sick, too?

A sick mother *and* a sick girlfriend?

But Carly's not my girlfriend...

I barely know her, except that she runs hot for me and is so easily aroused that she'd have come after a few more seconds if Chance hadn't disturbed us.

Still, concern for her wellbeing overwhelms me and threatens to rip my heart right out of my chest. I don't understand this emotion, this... protectiveness. It's swift and fierce. I protect all women, but this feeling for Carly's different. More.

"That's just it," Chance says. "She needs more than the one nighter my so-called brother plans to offer her."

That's what I want. *Wanted*. Still, I don't like the way it sounds when Chance mentions it. I had my fingers inside her. Felt the way she came alive around them. I'm not sure any longer that a quickie against the side of the bar will be enough.

"Isn't that for her to say?" Lexie asks. "And so what if she does? Can't a woman—even Carly—want a little fun?"

"Wait, wait, wait," another woman intervenes— Amanda, I think. She tucks her hair behind her ear. "This isn't right. I don't know Carly very well, but I don't think she'd be at all comfortable with the three of you talking about her like this when she isn't here."

I nod. Finally, someone with a level head. "You're right.

But you need to tell me one thing. Please. What is Carly healing from? Did she have cancer or something?"

Silence.

I swear to God I could hear a freaking pin drop.

"What? I know I just met her, but I like her. I'm concerned. How sick was she?"

I glance at Amanda first.

She shakes her head. "I don't know. I'm new in town, and I have no idea what they're talking about."

Lexie and Chance exchange glances.

Impatience rears its head. "I'll never hit a woman," I say, "Ever. Chance, though, I swear to God I'll give you the ass-whooping of a lifetime if you don't tell me what's going on."

Chance opens his mouth, but Lexie grabs his arm and shakes her head.

"No, Chance. It's not your story to tell."

"Damn it!" I raise my fist. "If she's sick, I need to know. I want to help her."

"She's not sick," Lexie says quietly. "She's just been through some...stuff."

"She's—"

Lexie cuts Chance off again. "No, Chance."

"Oh, for fuck's sake." I thread my fingers through my hair and leave them behind, stalking back into the bar. There's got to be someone who will tell me—

Then I see her.

Carly.

Walking out of the ladies' room, her face red and tear streaked, even in the bar's dim lighting.

Funny. The bar's nearly empty now. Where did everyone go? And why?

I walk slowly toward Carly. She doesn't run off, so that's a good sign. My fingers are still wet from her pussy, but I'm well aware that the fun's over. "Hey. You okay?"

She nods, trying to look everywhere but at me. "Fine. I'm getting out of here."

"Okay. I'll take you home."

She shakes her head. "No. Lexie's the designated driver. She'll take me."

"She's still outside," I explain.

Carly inhales a deep breath. "I just wish..."

"What? What do you wish, Carly?"

"That things were different." She chews on her lower lip. "I should have never come back to Bayfield. It made sense at the time, but I should have gone somewhere new, where I could reinvent myself. Where no one knows..."

My fingers itch. They itch to reach toward her, stroke her soft cheek. To wipe away the remnants of her tears. To caress her swollen lips, the fine curves of her neck. To continue where we were interrupted and see her let go.

To give her what she clearly wants.

But I force them to stay still.

"Where no one knows what?" I ask.

She drops her jaw. "They didn't tell you?" She lets out a soft huff. "I guess I should have known. Otherwise you'd be running in the other direction."

I frown. How bad could it be? "I wouldn't do that."

"Oh, you will. But you know what, Austin?" She glances around the bar. "I've already managed to clear out this place, and on ladies' night too. They aren't going to want me coming back here anytime soon. I don't really feel like talking about it. Especially to you." She whisks past me and out the door.

I move to follow her, but someone grabs my shoulder.

I turn.

Miles stands behind me.

"Where the hell have *you* been?" I ask.

"I was trying to have a quickie with a hot little redhead, but it got cut short when your girlfriend there—"

"*Not* my girlfriend." Damn. Why does it feel so wrong to say that?

He shrugs. "Whatever. She came into the bathroom crying, and it kind of spoiled the mood. So Robin and I left as discreetly as we could."

"A quickie in the ladies' room? Really?" I shouldn't be too bitter since I was just fingering Carly and getting her to come.

"All in fun. She was game. I think she's got a bit of an exhibitionist streak."

The corner of his mouth tips up and I can't help but wonder if he does too. Not that I give a shit.

"Sorry you got interrupted."

"Not a problem. She talked too much anyway." Miles sighs. "And speaking of talking, she told me a few things, *brother*. A few things you should know."

Miles doesn't have the same issue as Lexie does with gossip and gives me a fucking earful.

————

Two years ago, news broke that Manhattan billionaire Derek Wolfe had been murdered, and soon after, dozens of presumed dead young women were rescued from a private island in the South Pacific.

I paid little attention to the story at the time. Not because it wasn't totally fucked up, but because Mom had just been diagnosed with MS and our health insurer was giving us grief. It was a heartbreaking tale, but I didn't stop to think about it. Instead, I started working twice the hours since Mom could no longer fly with multiple sclerosis. I had more important things on my mind than a billionaire's murder and a bunch of young women I didn't know.

Except I do know one of them. Holy fuck.

Her name is Carly Vance, and...

I can't even.

Talk about dodging a bullet when Chance interrupted us.

Except...Carly was into it—into what we were doing. She's the one who kissed me! She started it, her pussy had been dripping wet and she almost came all over my fingers...

"Robin must be mistaken," I say.

"No. She's not," Miles's lips turn down. "Nearly everyone in town knows about Carly, about what happened to her. They thought she was dead, man. She's been home for a year living with her parents."

I can't let my mind go to what must have happened to her—sweet and beautiful Carly—on that island.

I want to hear her call my name when she comes, but she needs so much more than the orgasms and fund I can give her.

Chance is right. Carly deserves more than a quick kiss and finger against the wall outside a bar.

So much more.

As much as I want her—and God, I *do* want her—I'm not the man for her. I'm just passing through Montana. I'm only here because of the will, because of the money. I'll be gone as soon as that obligation has been met.

As for Carly... hell, I don't even *know* what she needs. Sure, a little while ago she needed an orgasm, but that's fleeting, no matter how talented my fingers are.

One thing I *can* do, though, is apologize—tell her how sorry I am that I took her in such a disrespectful way. Because a woman who's been through what she has deserves to feel safe.

"You okay, man?" Miles's voice breaks into my thoughts.

"Yeah." What a good liar I am.

"I know we don't know shit about each other, but I'd say you don't look okay."

Maybe not such a good liar after all.

I sigh, rub a hand down my face. Smell her on my fingers. My dick hardens at the instant thought of how her pussy clenched around them. How she'd held onto my wrist, kept me in place between her thighs.

"I need to talk to her. To Carly."

"You sure?"

"Yeah. I'm sure. Do you know where she lives?"

He frowns. "Hell, no. I just got here today, remember? Without the town laid out in a grid pattern with stoplights and street names, I'm fucking lost."

I sigh again. "Right. Of course you don't know. I'm not thinking straight. And no way will Chance tell me."

"There's this thing called the Internet," Miles says.

"And this is a small town. I swear the entire place could fit inside Madison Square Garden. Anyone who's lived here for more than a minute could probably tell you. But is that really a good idea?"

"I have no clue," I say, "but I have to. I just have to."

Miles glances at the doorway. "*He* might have something to say about that."

I don't even have to look. Already I know Chance has entered the bar.

"Nice going." He stalks over, scowling. "You seem to have turned ladies' night into a black hole."

I turn, instead of glancing over my shoulder, and face him. "Fuck you." I brush past him.

"She's gone," he calls. "Lexie took her home."

I ignore him.

"Come on, man," Miles calls. "Whatever you need to do can wait. She works at the ranch, after all. Have a drink with us."

"I'm done drinking for the night." I stride out the door of the bar and into the warm Montana summer air.

Chance drove us, so I'm walking. Where? No fucking clue. Does Carly live in town? Or does her family own one of the smaller ranches on the outskirts? She mentioned learning how to care for horses from her dad, so the family probably has some acreage.

I have no idea though.

I know nothing about this woman, and at the same time, I know everything about her. Everything she's been through. If that Wolfe fucker weren't dead, I'd track him down and kill him all over again.

And the worst part? I know I should have handled things with her differently. She's better off without me. I'll apologize and give her room. It's a big ranch and that can easily be accomplished.

I'm not good enough for her. I'm not sticking around. I have one woman to worry about. My mom. Maybe I'm a dick, but it's better now if she sees me that way. She can find a man who will treat her like a queen.

Yep, I sure dodged that gorgeous bullet.

Except...why does the idea of never seeing those green eyes light up or go hazy with passion again really piss me off? Why does the idea of some other man on the receiving end of those looks make me want to break some shit?

Maybe I didn't dodge it after all. It sure feels like a bullet is lodged right in the center of my heart—in the shape of Carly Vance.

8

 ARLY

"I TRIED WHEN I GOT HOME," I tell Dr. Lake the next day at our video chat session before my workday begins, "but I couldn't recapture the feeling. It was like the vibrator had lost its magic."

"The vibrator was never magic, Carly."

"You know what I mean. I couldn't"—I swallow—"finish." My cheeks are on fire.

"The vibrator was never supposed to be a substitute for the feelings an actual person can invoke in you," Dr. Lake says. "It was only to let you learn pleasure by your own hand, that your body isn't broken. That—"

"I know," I interrupt. "You've told me this over and over. It's just... I felt something amazing. Truly amazing, and then it got ruined. Everyone knows about me here. I couldn't have just *one* moment. One perfect moment before reality broke through." I shake my head. "I... think I need to leave Bayfield."

Dr. Lake nods. "It's an option. What do your parents think?"

I huff. "It's my decision, not theirs."

She's quiet for a moment. "That's true. You're twenty-seven, not sixteen. Still, it would be a shock to them to have you move away."

I roll my eyes, envisioning that fun conversation. "I already know what they think, so I haven't told them."

Dr. Lake smiles. "They only want what's best for you. They love you."

"I know that, and I love them for it, but last night proved that I can't be myself here. Austin didn't know anything about me. He just thought I was a woman who wanted sex. Nothing more. I'm sure he's been told the truth by now and now he's... *tainted* by it, just like everyone else. Just like *me*. I can't be the Carly I want to be here."

"You can't run away from what happened."

"I know that. God, do I know that. But no one will let me move on in a town this small. Last night was proof.

Chance Bridger interrupted us, stood up for me, and punched his half brother in the face. Because of me and my issues. Then..."

I laugh and rub a hand down my face.

"Then a crowd formed. They knew what was up. Why we were around the side of the bar. I feel like I'm in a soap opera and they got the first glimpse of a new season."

"It sounds really embarrassing."

"I'm surprised people didn't have popcorn."

Dr. Lake offers a small laugh, and I do, too. I'm not usually into dark humor, but it seems to work in this instance.

"I need to move forward, and..."

"And...?" Dr. Lake prompts.

"I never thought I could want a man after what I've been through, but I wanted this one. I wanted him like I've never wanted any man. Even before. I've never been this intensely attracted to someone."

"Then why are you thinking about leaving Bayfield?"

"Because by now, I'm sure he knows everything, and he's not going to want to have anything to do with me."

"Don't you think that's his decision to make?"

"His brother told him to keep his hands off me." I let out a sigh. "And that's the whole problem. Everyone—not just my parents—thinks they need to protect me. The head vet at the ranch had me grooming horses and feeding puppies yesterday. Puppies! I enjoyed it, but my *God*, I feel like I'm in a cage here, and I spent three years being held captive. That's more than enough for a lifetime."

"I understand, but I'm going to be honest with you." Dr. Lake sets down her notepad.

Uh-oh. When Dr. Lake puts down her notepad, she drops a bomb. Always.

"I don't think leaving Bayfield is a good idea."

"Why not?"

"Because this is your home, first of all."

"So what? This is also where I was taken, where my funeral was. Where I came back from the dead. No one knows how to deal with someone who does that. Everyone's afraid of what one little thing might do to me. They're all afraid I'm going to break. And I'm not going to break. I know that now."

"So *show* them that."

"Why is it all on me? Why shouldn't *they* try harder?" I shake my head. "I want to leave. I need to leave."

"Let me give you another reason to stay, then," Dr. Lake says.

I sigh. "Fine. Lay it on me."

"This man. Austin. If he's awakened something in you, do you really want to walk away from that?"

No. I don't want to walk away from that. But Austin

undoubtedly knows my story by now, and he won't want me anymore. He'll be glad if I leave quietly, especially since I'll be working on his ranch where he'll be for the next year. Then he won't have to make up some sorry excuse for why he doesn't want to see me. Or duck around horse stalls to steer clear. He can't leave, but *I* can.

"Besides," Dr. Lake continues, "there's one thing on your list you haven't accomplished yet."

She's right.

I've done everything else she's asked, including purchasing a vibrator—getting that past Mom was interesting—and giving myself an orgasm.

Except...

I haven't gone back to Millie's.

Millie's Diner, where I was having lunch when... when I was taken.

"Fine," I say. "I'll go."

I remember the scent of greasy French fries. The feel of the sticky fake leather bench seat. And more.

"Oh?"

I nod. "Yeah. I'll go to Millie's soon. Sometime within the week if I can. I'm strong enough. And once that's done, I'll begin researching places to relocate because Austin Bridger's going to want nothing to do with me now that he's learned about the *broken* Carly Vance."

"Carly..."

"I'm sorry, Dr. Lake." I glance at my watch. "I have to go. I'm going to be late for work."

———

LEXIE GIVES me some better tasks today, thank God, but not before she gives me the pitying look and asks three times if I'm okay after last night. She had a front row seat to that disaster.

I assure her I'm fine, and then she shows me how to take the livestock's vitals and record everything on an iPad. We take the ATVs out into the fields and walk up to the Herefords as they graze. It's hot, and my hat may shield my face from the sun, but it's sweaty work. That keeps me busy until lunchtime, and I know just where I want to spend the hour.

Right at the edge of the Bridger property is a small freshwater spring. Whether the Bridgers actually own it, I don't know. I stumbled across it when I first returned to Bayfield after my year of intensive therapy.

Walking was my solace then, and though at first I was a bit fearful of being alone, I got over my qualms quickly, especially in a place like this. It gave me time to think, and I ended up strolling miles and miles each day...and that's how I found my secret spring.

I doubt that it's truly a secret, but I've never seen

anyone else there. I stop in the vet's office in the stable and wash up, and—

"Hi, Carly."

I don't have to turn around. I'd know that deep voice anywhere. My heart skips a beat and I'm instantly hot all over. I'm not sure if it's from desire or embarrassment over the night before.

I turn off the faucet. "Austin."

Why is his name so breathy?

I turn, ready to apologize. Or run. Or jump him. I'm not sure which. Instead of any of those, I let out a laugh.

He's dressed in tattered jeans, a plain white T-shirt—although it's not all that white any longer—and brown boots. Army boots maybe? They're not cowboy boots and they're filthy. His face is shiny with sweat and his gorgeous dark hair is plastered to his temples. He sports a purplish bruise on his sculpted jawline where Chance clocked him last night.

"What's so funny?" He glances down at himself.

"You look...worn."

He lifts his head and frowns. "Chance had me up at six. Miles and I have been mending fences all morning."

"Don't you have people to do that?"

"Hell, yeah, we have people to do that. Lots of ranch hands. But..." He shakes his head. "It's a long and boring story about how I'm now a cowboy-in-training, and I'd much rather talk about you. Are you all right?"

"Why wouldn't I be?"

My question is ridiculous, of course. I left the bar last night without a word to him after yelling at the entire crowd. All this *after* he had his hand in my panties, his fingers working me like an expert and getting me to the brink.

He thinks I'm a mess.

In many ways, I am. Especially when it comes to men. Specifically him.

But these are my issues and I can't let him feel guilty. He didn't do anything wrong. Neither of us did, even though I'm still slightly mortified.

"I just..." He shoves his hands in the pockets of his jeans and looks down. "I'm sorry, Carly."

My stomach drops, right along with all hope and expectation of things with Austin being different. Right. Here it comes. "For what, exactly?"

He lifts his gaze, but not his head, so his dark eyes meet mine through his ridiculously long man-lashes. "I didn't know. If I'd known, I never would have—"

I want to stomp my foot in frustration, like a toddler. Instead, I set my hands on my hips. "Which is exactly why I didn't want you to know, Austin. I'm not ashamed of what we did, and you shouldn't be either."

I'm embarrassed that Chance caught us and that everyone in the bar knew what we'd been up to, but I'm not at all ashamed of what we did together.

He pops his head up and his eyes widen. "Ashamed? Carly, I'm not ashamed. I…" He snaps his mouth shut as he runs a hand over the back of his neck.

Is he nervous? Confused? Well, so am I.

"What?"

"I like you, a lot. I just…"

"Oh, for God's sake." I brush past him because he sounds like a thirteen-year-old. I don't want that. I want a man. The guy who had me pressed against the side of the bar, his fingers inside me. Pointing out how wet I was for him. How eager. "I'm going to lunch."

His long strides overtake me in an instant, and he stands between me and the office door. He's so big he practically fills the space. I can't get around him and I should feel threatened, but instead, I just feel small. Feminine.

"Please. Talk to me."

I have to tip my chin up to look into his dark eyes so he can see the annoyance in mine. I set my arms across my chest and fortify myself for the same old argument. I only hoped I wouldn't have to do it with him. "About what? About how broken I am and why I shouldn't be letting strange men into my pants outside a bar at night? Thanks, but no."

"Carly…" My name comes out of him like a groan.

I purse my lips and tap my toe on the floor. "I only have an hour for lunch. Now get out of my way."

He grins. "You can have as long as you want for lunch. Seems I'm your boss."

I shake my head. "Lexie's my boss. And I will only take an hour. I take this position seriously. I need it."

I'm not going to tell him it's for more than money. I need the experience…and the independence. The freedom.

He relaxes, his demeanor changing to something more confident. "Then let me join you. Please. I want to talk."

"I told you—"

"It doesn't have to be about that."

"Then about what?"

He shrugs those broad shoulders. I remember how hard and sculpted his muscles were beneath my palms the night before.

"Anything. I want to know you."

I cock my head, debating if he's being sincere. "I'm sure your brother told you all about me, after he warned you to keep your distance."

Austin laughs then, sounding more like a cowboy than a city boy from Seattle. "I don't take orders from Chance. I figure you're the only one who can tell me to stay away. I'll respect *your* wishes, but fuck anyone else who keeps me from you."

A smile edges to my lips. He said just the right thing, and I'm betting Austin Bridger doesn't take orders from anyone.

"That bruise on your jaw says otherwise," I remind him.

He absently glides his fingers over the contusion. "It'll take more than that."

And that right there makes him all the more attractive. He makes the walls I build to protect myself start to crumble. I'll be cautious, but I like how it feels to let him in, even if it's only a little bit.

I want to get to know him, too. I haven't stopped. I bite my lip and study him. He's patient as I think on it, as if waiting for me to tell him to fuck off. To leave me alone.

"I'm not weak," I say instead. "I'm broken, but I'm fixing myself."

"Carly, you're not br—"

I hold up a hand. "I am. I'm broken, but I'm getting better. A little at a time. Last night..." I roll my eyes. "God, last night helped with that a lot. Because you thought I was just Carly. Not Broken Carly like Chance thinks of me. Like Lexie and the entire town."

He sighs and reaches out and strokes a hand over my

hair, tucks some strands that have come loose behind my ear. "Baby, shh."

Pet names. I don't like them. But I no longer seem to mind.

I close my eyes and revel in the feel. In his lack of more words.

When he drops his hand, I look up at him. Does he know about the hidden spring? Probably not, since he only arrived a few days ago. Funny. I didn't want to share that place with anyone.

Except now I do.

I want to share it with Austin. Want to share *more* with him.

"Okay. Come on," I say. "I want to show you something. We have to drive for about ten minutes to get there."

He steps back to let me out of the room. "Drive into town?"

I step out into the central hallway of the stable. The tang of horses is stronger out here. The sliding doors are open at either end of the building, allowing natural light and fresh summer air in.

"No. To the edge of your property."

"Can't we just walk?"

I laugh then. A big belly laugh, and damn, it feels good. "You have no idea how large your ranch is, do you? Come on. I've got a secret to share."

 USTIN

I'VE GOT a secret to share, she said. I didn't expect this.

I'm in awe.

When I first learned to fly and had a birds eye view of the sky from the cockpit of a small plane, I fell in love with its beauty. Even during a storm, it's still magnificent, with its blues, grays, and subtle greens. Flashes of lightning. Then after a storm, when a rainbow is visible from high above. Incredible.

Nature is awe inspiring.

I've never felt quite the same way about anything on the ground. Oh, I love the coasts and the mountains as much as anyone, but seeing it all from above... there's nothing quite like it.

Until now.

Carly stops the car at a random spot on the side of a dirt road and then we walk about a quarter mile to a small clearing.

Now I'm gaping. Fucking gaping at the majesty before me.

"Holy shit."

I see out of the corner of my eye that Carly grins.

A small waterfall splashes down gray rock and into a pool. The overflow trickles down into the lush grass in a wandering, slow path. Tiny evergreen trees sprout up from the dirt between the stones, and a large cottonwood offers some shade. Yet this water source isn't part of the creek. It's separate, as if it magically comes from the ground. A spring.

It's pure splendor...yet it pales in comparison to Carly. How, here at her secret place, she looks happy. Content. Like her troubles and *brokenness* melt away.

She's wearing her sable hair up in a high ponytail, which accents her perfect cheekbones and ears graced only with the tiniest gold studs. Her green T-shirt is tight, showing her curves—God, those amazing tits—and her ass is as delectable as ever in bootcut denim.

And then...her eyes. Emerald green with flecks of gold.

What is it about her that's so intriguing? That has me thinking of her all the time? That has me wanting her body, but also her heart? I want to protect her from everything I learned from Miles but know I can't. Fuck. She was taken. Stolen. Held against her will by some sick fuck for several years.

Carly may not know it, but she has a spine of steel to have survived something like that and still be sweet enough to show me this perfect spot. She's at peace here, and fuck if I don't want to always see her smile like she is right now.

She gave this spot to me as a gift. I want to give her gifts like this in return, but I don't know how. I'm barely a cowboy. I'm a fly boy who's grounded.

Still, she brought *me* here. Me. Not Miles. Not Chance. Me.

"Where does this come from?" I crouch down to look closely.

She shrugs and looks off into the distance. "Beats me. My best guess is that it's an offshoot from Big Salmon Creek. I tried to follow it once, but the terrain gets too rocky in places." She leans down and pools some of the clear water in her hands. "It's fresh and cool. I've always wanted to taste it, but I haven't."

"Man, I could sure use a dowsing after the morning I've had." I stand and pull my T-shirt over my head without thought.

Carly's eyes widen at my chest.

"Oh." I shove the T-shirt back on. "I'm sorry." Shit. I fucked it up.

"For what?" Her eyes are wide and she licks her lips. "You look amazing. Take it off, Austin. Get in. I agree, you're a mess. Rinse off."

I'm unsure, because what if I somehow push her too far without even touching her? I had my hands on her the other night and she was fine. But what Miles said...

She seems fine. Gave me consent to continue.

I decide to wing it. She's not a nun who hasn't seen a bare chest before. "I've got to tell you," I admit, "a shower under that waterfall sounds like heaven." I sit down on a small boulder and peel off my boots and socks. I'm ready to strip off the jeans and skivvies, when I turn to Carly. "You okay?"

She huffs. "I wish people would stop asking me that. I'm fine. Please don't be one of them, Austin. Take it off. Take it *all* off."

Then she laughs, and I swear to God it's the sweetest sound I've ever heard. Sweeter even than the rushing water.

I remove my jeans but stop at my forest green boxer

briefs, totally aware of my hardening cock, because when a woman says *take it all off,* a man's going to get fucking hard. When it's Carly and she's watching me? Fuck.

I step into the pool. Boxers on.

It's cool but not freezing. Perfect. I walk in farther, and the water hits me right above my waist. I splash some over my chest and face, and then I stride to the waterfall.

I let out a small groan and close my eyes. It's quite a bit colder than the standing water. But damn it feels good, and it also takes care of my erection problem.

Not for long, though.

"How is it?" Carly yells above the rush of the fall.

"It's amazing. You should come in." Shit. Bad move. "Or not. I didn't mean—"

"Oh, shut up, Austin. I'm coming in. I didn't come all this way to look at the water."

I glance away to give her privacy even though I want to watch her more than I want my next breath.

Until I can't help myself.

I step out of the fall, rub the water out of my eyes, and take a good long look because I'm only a man and she's...

Fuck.

Her bra.

She's not wearing it. In fact, it's on the soft grass along with the rest of her clothes. Her gorgeous tits are on full display as she walks into the pool wearing only white cotton panties. They're not racy in any way, but they're the sexiest pair I've ever laid eyes on. The temperature of the water has forced her nipples into erect nubs, and—

Damn. The water no longer has any power over my loins. It's as if she was made for me. Petite, lush curves. A narrow waist but wide hips. Muscled thighs that I imagine gripping my waist as I fuck her. A full ass I want to grab and... Would she go for a spanking? She's such a good girl in those innocent little panties.

She's not trying. No seduction. No practiced wiles. In fact, she stumbles a little. Instead of making her seem clumsy, it's erotic as hell the way her breasts sway.

I want to punish her for making me helpless to her.

I'm hard as a fucking rock even with my dick submerged.

I can't help the groan that escapes. "Baby, fuck, you're perfect."

She flows toward me, her motions languid, as if she's a mermaid. Only she's more beautiful than any siren of the sea.

She's...

She's fucking spectacular.

My fingers tingle. They tingle to reach out and cup those perfect breasts. Tingle to feel the inside of her tight warm pussy again.

Tingle to touch every fucking inch of her.

And knowing I can't. I shouldn't.

Until—

She reaches toward me and caresses my shoulder with her small hand. Glides her magic fingers down my arm to my hand that's beneath the water. I have no idea what she's up to, but she...

Oh, God...

She lifts it and places it on her breast.

"Baby," I groan, reveling in the soft feel of her.

I don't do anything except breathe, and I'm not sure if I'm even doing that. I had my hand on her last night and she was liquid fire. Heat. Passion. Until we were interrupted. Until the world butted into something that was just the two of us.

We're alone now. Carly and me. Just us. Only a pair of panties and boxer briefs keeping my dick from sinking into her. She'll be so hot around me compared to the cool water. Responsive. Hopefully a little wild.

"I—"

"Touch me, Austin," she all but begs, cutting off my last bit of resistance. "Please touch me."

I'm strong, but I'm only a man. It'll take more than a punch from Chance to keep me from her now.

 ARLY

DESPITE BEING in the cool water, Austin's palm is warm against my flesh. I close my eyes and let out a soft sigh.

He can't see my scars. Not yet. They're mostly on my inner thighs, but there are a few on my back. He may see them when we get out of the spring, but I can't worry about that now. Not when his strong hand is cupping me so delectably.

He jerks his hand away. "Carly..."

I pop my eyes open. "Damn it. I know you like me. I know you want me."

He groans. "God, I do. But baby, the last thing I ever want to do is hurt you."

"Did you hurt me last night when you had your fingers inside me?"

"I—"

"I'll answer for you. You didn't, Austin. You didn't hurt me. You made me *feel*. And God, it's been so long."

His resistance crumbles. He grabs me then, pulls me into his embrace. Instead of his lips meeting mine, though, they brush against my forehead. "Carly...I want you so much, but fuck. We need to talk first."

A quick roll of his hips and I come in contact with the proof of his desire, but the seriousness in his gaze has me stilling.

"About what?" I ask cautiously.

"About what happened to you. I know you want me to treat you like nothing happened, but we're going to do things that might... I don't know what."

I look at his chest and run my fingertips over the skin. "I was taken from the diner in town. Millie's. Kidnapped. I was held for three years on an island and —" I swallow, trying not to let the memories mess with where we are.

"What did they do to you?"

I blink and then swirl my finger through the smattering of hair on his broad chest. "*Everything.*"

I'm not telling him more. Not now. Not like this when we're so close.

He sighs and his fingers clench where they hold me. This is where he'll reject me, carry me out of the water and cover me up. I hold my breath and wait.

"Then tell me," he says finally. "Tell me what to do. You be in charge."

I whip my head up and stare at him. He wants to continue? Relief courses through me, along with excitement.

"I don't want to be in charge. Before I was taken, I liked a man to...to be a man. A little dominant, a little rough because he couldn't help himself. That I aroused him enough to lose his mind a little. It was powerful."

Being in charge *would* make me feel powerful. Austin isn't wrong. But more than that, I want to watch him lose control in me.

I look into his eyes—those deep brown eyes. "Take me. Right here in this spring. Right here in this special place that I've never shared with anyone. I didn't have to bring you here, Austin. I wanted to. It was my choice. And this is also my choice."

He pulls back and trails his finger lightly over my cheek, lower to my shoulder, and then further to my breast. He circles my hard nipple. "I want to go slowly."

"For God's sake," I huff.

Then he pinches the tip, and I gasp.

"Slow doesn't mean I won't please you." His voice is deep and a bit bossy.

The little bite of pain has me clenching my thighs together, as if my nipples and my pussy are connected.

"You deserve better than a quick fuck. Our first time won't be rushed. I have plans for you and I need hours to work through even a fraction of them."

Hours?

"But you didn't want slow last night. Before you knew the truth about me," I counter.

He meets my gaze, nearly melting me. "I wanted to make you come. To watch you let go. I wouldn't have fucked you against the side of the building."

"I wanted that," I admit. "I was ready. I *am* ready."

"Have you been with a man since you returned?"

I blink at the question. Not because of what he asked, but the simple fact that he asked it. Everyone else avoids the elephant in the room. I respect him for it and I want to answer.

"No. No one's touched me like that since I've been back. Until last night. With you."

"I sure as hell am not rushing this then. I want to take my time with you. The anticipation is...foreplay."

I look into his dark eyes that are heavy lidded with arousal. And I see...truth. He believes what he says.

"I want to come," I pout. I sound like a child who was taken to an ice cream shop but not given a cone.

He kisses my lips this time—just a simple peck, but it jolts straight between my legs. Then his mouth is on me, tongue finding mine. Licking into me. I whimper at the feel of him. The need that practically vibrates through the water.

"We were interrupted last night, weren't we?"

I nod, rolling my hips with eagerness for what we did.

Slowly, he slides his hand down my body and between my legs. "You want me to touch you here again?"

He glides his fingers over my panties and the heat of it—even in the cool water—is striking.

I grip his biceps.

"Please," I beg, my pussy clenching.

He slips beneath the edge of my panties and finds my center. I'm wet for him—and not from the pool of water—and his fingers sink into me easily. I go up on my tiptoes as he does something magical.

"Austin!" I cry out.

"You're clenching me so tight. You have a greedy pussy, baby."

I do. I so do, for Austin. And his fingers. And his thumb which now circles my swollen clit.

Just like that, so fast... "Oh God, I'm going to come."

He brings me to the brink so easily. He doesn't

torment me at all, just quickly and thoroughly pushes me over into my first manmade orgasm in... ever.

"Yes!" I practically scream, pleasure coursing through me more than I ever imagined.

Austin whispers dirty things in my ear as I clench around his fingers deep inside me. Only when I set my forehead on his chest does he still and then slip out from me.

"Prettiest fucking thing I've ever seen," he murmurs.

I have to smile because I'm satisfied and relaxed. Content and in a handsome man's arms. I reach between us to reciprocate, but he takes my hand and raises it to his lips. Kisses the wet knuckles.

"I need a bed and hours of time for what I want to do to you."

I have to nod, but I can feel the hard prod of him as he tips my chin up to kiss me.

"I understand better now." He pulls away and rests his forehead against mine. "Thank you for sharing, so now it's my turn to share too."

I lean into him and brush my lips over his chest and the smattering of dark hair. "All right," I sigh. "I'd love to know you better. But even though you don't want me to touch you, you can still touch me while you share."

He laughs and lifts his hands—both of them—back to my breasts.

God, yes.

As we stand close, the still water surrounding us, he talks to me. No, he talks to my breasts, his gaze focused on his hands cupping them. His thumbs sliding over the nipples. He weighs them, kneads them, caresses them, all the while the sound of the waterfall is like a shield, blocking out the outside world.

I'm in a dazed state of sexual bliss and simmering arousal.

He talks to me about his home in Seattle. About his seaplane business. About flying and how much he loves it.

And then his voice softens, and he tells me about his mother, Diana Lovering.

His mother, who was diagnosed with multiple sclerosis and who can no longer fly the planes she loves.

"I'll do anything for her," he says. "Even live on this ranch for a year, because it means I'll go home a billionaire and—"

"Wait, what?" I lift my head to meet his eyes.

I had no idea my breasts are so sensitive, that I could get close to coming from just his thorough touch. His hands haven't left them, haven't dipped lower. I'm achy and needy all over again and it's hard to focus.

"That's why you have to stay here?"

He nods. "My father's will has the three of us inheriting evenly. With the stipulation that Miles and I live here at Bridger Ranch for a year first."

I blink. I knew the Bridgers had money. Their property is too impressive for them to be anything but ridiculously rich. But *billionaires?*

"Mom will have everything she needs to live a happy and fulfilled life for as many years as she has left." His hands finally fall away.

Maybe it's because he's talking about his mother and feeling me up at the same time. Maybe he's getting as worked up as me.

"What will you do while you're here then? I mean, you're not a cowboy."

I take his hand and pull it back to touch me again, but he redirects me, setting my hand this time on his chest. He's giving me permission to touch him, to learn him, too.

He raises a brow as if I've offended him. "If Chance has his way, Miles and I will be whipped into shape before the month's out."

"Don't you miss flying?" I brush my fingers over one of his flat nipples.

His breath catches. "Hell, yeah. But working the land doesn't suck all that much. Maybe it's the Bridger blood in me."

I lean into him, relish his muscled body, and I *feel*. The

heat of his skin. The hard play of muscle and bone beneath.

I feel so much, only it's not purely physical this time.

This time, it's—

I pull back quickly. "Shit!"

His body stiffens and he looks around. "What's wrong?"

"How long have we been gone? I have to get back to work. This is only my second day. I'm going to get my ass fired."

"It's okay." He winks and relaxes. "I know your boss."

"Austin, no. I told you I'm not going to play that card. Come on." I wade out of the water, mindful of my faint scars and wishing for a towel.

"Baby," he groans.

"Don't *baby* me. I have a job and I'm serious about it."

Still, I'm disappointed. I liked having my hands on him. I liked his hands on *me* even more.

I wipe as much wetness off me as I can and hastily don my clothes before he can notice the scarring. At least my hair is dry. I didn't go under the waterfall with him.

He doesn't say anything further. Doesn't belittle my job or my desire to get back to it. Quietly, he dresses as well. We get into the car and head back to the vets' office on the ranch. No sooner are we parked than I exit without saying goodbye and run in.

"Lexie?"

I breathe a sigh of relief. She's not back from lunch yet, and it turns out I'm only five minutes late. I head back outside to say goodbye to Austin.

But he's gone. Shit.

———————

"CARLY," Dad says at dinner, "I need to talk to you about the Bridgers."

Mom made meatloaf, one of my dad's favorites. He uses his fork to break off a piece.

"I'm not quitting, Dad." I reach for my iced tea and take a deep sip.

I only saw Lexie briefly after lunch since she went out with one of the ranch hands to see to a sick calf. I stayed in the stables and dealt with the horses, my mind well filled with thoughts about Austin and how I liked his touch. How I wanted more of it. Except he disappeared. Did I do something to mess it all up? In my rush, I didn't say goodbye.

Dad breaks me from my thoughts. "It's not about that."

Inwardly, I sigh with relief. "Oh. All right. What is it?"

"Rick, do we have to do this now?" Mom stirs her peas around on her plate. She's worried about another argument.

"I'm sorry, sweetie, but yes," Dad tells her. "She needs to know. Especially if she thinks she's going to work at that ranch."

I wrinkle my forehead and don't miss the way he spits out *that ranch*. "Know what?"

"Did you ever wonder why I decided to run for mayor of Bayfield?"

I offer a shrug. "I figured you wanted to be more involved in the town." I bite on my lip. "I'm sorry. I should have asked. I've been in my own head since I got home."

"Carly, honey, I didn't bring this up to make you feel guilty," Dad says. "You needed to focus on your healing. But now that you're working for the Bridgers, there are things you should know."

"I know all I need."

He shakes his head. "You don't. For example, did you know that the Bridger family owns our ranch?'

I raise my eyebrows, stare at him as if he said the property is owned by space aliens. "What?"

He nods. "It's true. We—your mother and I—ran into some financial difficulties while you were gone, as you know."

A sick feeling settles in my stomach and I set down my fork. "I know you had to sell the animals, and I'm so sorry for that."

His face softens. "Sweetheart, no. This isn't for you to

feel guilty. I would have sold the shirt off my back to find you."

I purse my lips. "It sounds like you nearly did."

"If it would have done any good, I would have. When your mother and I made the decision to sell the land, we engaged a real estate broker in Helena to list it. It turned out she was on Jonathan Bridger's payroll."

I'm confused. "I don't understand."

"We didn't know it at the time, but she was working with Bridger to purchase as much land adjacent to his ranch as possible. She told us the offer was a good one, so we believed her, but we found out later that Bridger paid us only a little over half of what our property is worth."

I drop my mouth open. "Wait. You don't own this place? Why are we still living here?"

"I'm renting. One of the few perks of being mayor is that the city pays for my housing. Mom and I didn't want to leave our home, so the city attorney made a deal with Bridger that we could stay in the house. But we don't own it, and we can't use any of our property for ranching."

"I don't understand." I shake my head. "How could any of this happen? Your broker acted in bad faith. Don't you have some kind of remedy?"

"Sure. The law is on our side, but how would we pay an attorney to fight this? Bridger has unlimited funds. He'd have sent us to the poorhouse."

I shake my head. "Daddy, that was Jonathan Bridger. Not his sons."

Dad clenches his jaw, and his earlier softened features are now hardened. "I've said it before. The apple doesn't fall far from the tree, little one."

I meet my father's tired gaze. "So you ran for mayor for a paycheck?"

He sniffs. "Yes and no. We're not broke, but we were robbed. Now we're renters on our own land."

I'm sure there's more he's not telling me, as if he's forcefully holding the words back. My mom's quiet beside him. She doesn't offer up any more information.

Dad can't make much in such a small town. There must be some other reason.

"So I need you to leave that position, Carly," he says. "The Bridger family has taken enough from us."

"This isn't them taking from us. This is them *giving*. They gave me a job. A job doing what I love to do, taking care of animals. The money can help pay bills you have."

"I don't want any more Bridger money," he snaps. "You can take care of animals somewhere else. This is Bayfield. There are ranches everywhere."

"But they have amazing animals. I won't get that kind of experience anywhere else in the whole state of Montana!"

Dad forks a piece of meatloaf, takes a bite, chews,

swallows. Then he looks at me calmly. "This discussion is over. You will give your notice in the morning."

Dad's issues with Jonathan Bridger are unfortunate. I'm mad for him. Angry. But the man's dead. I know Chance. I grew up with him. He protected me like a big brother from Austin. I don't know Miles much at all, but I am knowing more and more about Austin. He doesn't like Jonathan Bridger any more than my dad does.

I won't blanket blame like Dad because in the short time I've been working at Bridger Ranch, I've felt better. Stronger. Braver. Hell, even sexier.

I stand. Between missing lunch entirely and eating only two bites of my dinner, I should be hungry. But I'm too busy being angry.

"I will not quit. I'm a grown woman, and you can't make me."

"That makes you sound like you're seven," Dad counters.

I lean in. "How about this? No. Fucking. Way."

Mom gasps. I walk—despite my desire to run like the child he accused me of being—to my room and close my door, resisting the urge to slam it.

I wish I could talk to Austin about this. Austin, who I still barely know but feel close to—the operative word being *feel*.

I wish I could leave Bayfield, except...

Austin is here.

And God help me, I don't want to leave Austin. I want to see where it goes with us. I'm not expecting a marriage proposal, but a manmade orgasm and sex would be a good start.

I stopped crying a while ago.

But tonight, I cry.

Only a little, though, because a wave of determination sweeps through me.

I'm not quitting.

I love my father, but I'm not quitting.

Not on my job. Not on myself. Not on the chance of something with Austin Bridger.

USTIN

FOR TWO MORE DAYS, Chance keeps Miles and me busy from fucking dawn to dinner. Fortunately, he had us riding the never-ending fence line on ATVs instead of horses. He knows our limits. The repair check is something that can be done in the winter when there are fewer chores, although the snow's usually too deep, and it's fucking freezing. It's also something that can be done by ranch hands, not the property owners. But I'm thankful for the cowboy-warmup he's given us. He could have had us turning bull calves into steers by castrating them, but instead chose something involving a hammer and nails.

He kept us so occupied that I haven't seen Carly since our lunch break at the spring. Funny, we didn't eat lunch. We just talked. Rather, I talked—while playing with her perfect tits—and she seemed content to listen. It could have also been the fact that I made her come on my fingers first and then got to play with her perfect tits.

It was heaven and hell rolled into one.

I have blisters on my hands—and not just from jerking off solo in the shower to the image of Carly—and my back aches. I may have lost five pounds from sweating. I still have the fading bruise on my jaw from Chance's sucker punch the other night.

I need another opportunity to meet with Carly. Or an actual date. Anything where I can see her smile again. Watch her eyes go hazy with desire. Feel her nipples harden beneath my palms.

Neither Miles nor I pussied out with ranch work, so Chance seems to have some grumbling respect for us. Enough to invite us to head into town with him for supplies and a beer before another grueling round of fence repair.

We're bumping down the dirt road toward Bayfield when my mom calls. Chance's truck is new, shiny, and fucking huge. It's a four-door dually, meaning it has double wheels in the back that help haul heavy shit. The windows are down, and some country singer on the radio is crooning about front porches and short skirts.

"Hey," I say into my cell.

Chance gives me a glance from the driver's seat and turns down the music. Miles is in the back, his blond hair —which only three days ago was styled like a city slicker —catches the breeze.

"Hi, sweetheart. How's it going?" Mom asks.

"Good."

"Is everyone nice?"

I laugh. "It's not the first day of second grade. Don't worry, I've only gotten into one fight."

"What?"

I see Mom's face in my mind's eye. Her lips are parted into an O and her eyebrows have flown off her forehead. I took her looks instead of my father's. We have the same dark hair and eyes.

Chance raises a brow at me and I ignore him, looking out the side window as the prairie rushes by. I doubt Chance has forgiven me for touching Carly—not that I'm going to tell him shit about our time at the secret spring—but he hasn't thrown another punch either. He made his point and now I'm going to do what I fucking want. He might want to sucker punch me again, but I won't let him land another.

Since our time together at the spring, I looked for

Carly, cutting once through the stable like a teenager passing the cheerleader tryouts. She wasn't there. I hope she hasn't quit because of me. Probably not. I figure Chance would have said.

Since he hasn't, and my nose isn't broken, I figure he still likes me, or at least settled his issue with the punch. Hell, he's taking Miles and me for beers, so I'd say he doesn't hate me. For now.

Miles is cool and all, but I doubt we'll be getting mani-pedis together when the year is up. There wasn't much bonding at the bar the other night, and the workload Chance piled on us isn't a get-to-know-you vacation.

"I'm kidding," I say to Mom.

I'd rather she not worry. Besides, what kind of grown man tattles to Mommy about a bully on the playground?

Funny thing is, if our places were reversed? I'd have done the same thing as Chance. I'd protect a woman who's been through what Carly has, just as he did. Which means I grudgingly have to like the guy.

"Really. How is it? I still can't believe your father's doing this to you. And the other boys."

I mentally shrug because we've been over this before. "You know, you never talked much about him. Jonathan. In fact, not at all. I'm here now, so maybe you can give me some details."

She pauses a second and then sighs. "He's always been

part of my past. Until now, so I guess you're right. I was twenty-three and working at a bar to put myself through flight school. He came in and swept me off my feet."

"Just like that? I mean, you married him."

"I did. He was a nice man." She pauses. "Until he wasn't."

I still. I never heard her say that before. "He hurt you?"

Chance stiffens beside me.

"Sweetheart, it's old news. Thirty-five years, to be exact."

I shake my head even though she can't see. "It's not old news. I'm in Montana because he forced me here. Pretty much extortion. He's fucking with my life—and my brothers' lives—from the grave."

"I'm glad you're thinking of them as your brothers."

I frown. *Am* I thinking that? I clear the thought and get back to Mom.

"Besides divorcing you when you were pregnant, what did he do to you? I think I deserve to know now."

She sighs and is quiet for a minute.

"Mom," I prompt.

"Our relationship was a whirlwind. I know you don't want to hear about your mother's sex life, but I'll just say it was lust at first sight. Looking back, I have to wonder if it was ever love, at least for him. We married, and I moved to Montana."

"You stopped going to flight school?"

"I did." She gave up her dream because she got married.

"Then…"

"Then the real Jonathan Bridger showed himself. Verbal abuse. Drinking. Womanizing. He hit me once. Only once. I was pregnant with you and I told him the good news. That's why he hit me. Because I got *knocked up*. He divorced me before you were born."

"He didn't want kids," I muse.

My free hand is clenched into a fist, ready to beat the shit out of the dead man who laid a hand on my mom.

She sighs. "I returned to Seattle and got through flight school."

And never married again. It seems nothing, especially love, got in her way again. Once bitten—or beaten —twice shy.

"I'm sorry you married him," I tell her.

Her life could have turned out so differently if she'd never gotten involved with Jonathan Bridger.

"Oh, sweetheart. I'm not."

I set my elbow in the open window and lean my head into the phone. "Why the hell not? He was an asshole to you and didn't deserve you."

"Because he gave me you. I'd do it all over again."

I'm quiet because…fuck. My mom did everything for

me. Everything. Now she's sick and I'm far away and can't help.

I switch topics. "Your sink clogging again?"

"No, it's fine."

She pauses, and just when I'm about ready to break the silence—

"Sweetheart, sometimes bad things happen," she says, not taking the hint. "It's hard. Hell, even. But good things result from it. You can't often see it until later, when you look back. You are the best thing in my world, and as much as I hate to admit it, you were a gift from Jonathan Bridger. I'll always be grateful to him for giving me the person I love most. You gave my life purpose, Austin. You inspired me to fulfill my dreams."

Mom's words ring true. She always put me first, and I never went to bed not knowing I was cherished by the only parent who mattered.

I think of Carly, of what she went through, and wonder if she sees any good things that came from her hellish experience. How can she?

We ride into town and Chance pulls into a parking spot around the central square. It's a small park with what looks like a war memorial. The town looks more like Mayberry than Bayfield, where nothing bad ever happens.

"I have to go," I say. "Love you."

"Love you, too, sweetheart."

I end the call.

"Your mom?" Miles disconnects his seatbelt.

While we worked side by side the past two days, we didn't talk all that much.

Instead, Carly invaded my thoughts. The way she looked outside the bar as she rocked her hips onto my fingers. The feel of her hand clenching my wrist. How her eyes closed halfway as she was about to come. How I wanted to get her there, and did just that at the spring. I pushed her over and she was fucking gorgeous.

I let go of my dick-hardening thoughts of Carly and focus back on Miles's question. "Yeah. She's got MS and I worry, being so far away."

"She okay?" he asks.

I nod. "Yeah, it's in the early stages, but she can't fly any longer."

"She a pilot, too?" Chance takes off his sunglasses and tosses them on the dash.

"She started the seaplane company. Had to support herself—and me—after dear old Dad dumped her. She took all the flights when I was a kid. I got my pilot's license the second I was old enough and I've been working beside her ever since. I took over all the routes when she was grounded last year."

And the bills. And all the other shit.

"Now you're not there," Chance says.

"Nothing gets by you, does it? Now I'm not there. But she's hanging in there. So's the business with a guy who's filling in for me on the routes." *For now, anyway.*

"Sounds like your mom's a badass," Miles runs a hand over his scruffy jaw. "And our father's a dick."

"No shit."

Chance grabs his Stetson from the center console, opens his door but doesn't climb out until he says, "Our father *was* a dick."

I meet Miles's gaze after that truth bomb. Chance hasn't shared his feelings about anything other than Carly Vance. I assumed he's just a cranky fucker, but it seems there's more to it than two half brothers taking his hard-earned money.

I hop out and catch up to Chance on the sidewalk. "You lived with the guy. I thought you two were—"

Chance tips his head my way. "Close? Best buds?"

Miles is right on our heels.

"You two don't know shit," Chance snaps.

"Fine," Miles cuts in. "Then tell fucking tell us. You lost your dad. Regardless of what we think of him, I'm sure it's hard."

Chance laughs, but it's clear he's not amused.

"Is it about the money then?" I ask.

Chance stops on the sidewalk and crosses his arms.

"You think I care that you two take a cut? What the fuck am I going to do with *three* billion dollars?"

Donate it to charity? Pay off small business debts and buy a fleet of seaplanes? Pay for multiple sclerosis drugs and treatment programs?

"If it's not that," Miles says, "then what the hell crawled up your butt and died? I mean, are you cranky all the fucking time?"

Chance starts walking again and his long gait eats up the distance to the bar, but he slows. "Shit."

Miles and I look around. "What?"

"One of the many things that crawled up my butt and died, as you put it?" Chance rakes a hand down his face. "Him. Rick Vance."

I follow Chance's glare and glimpse an older man in pressed jeans and a crisp white snap shirt. He looks like he came out of a commercial for ironing starch. He's walking our way. I can tell the second he sees us, or at least Chance, because his entire demeanor shifts. To anger. Rage, even. His face turns ruddy, and if I were closer, I'd probably see a vein bulging in his neck. His hands are clenched into fists.

Yeah, this guy doesn't like Chance. Not one fucking bit.

Wait... *Vance.*

"You mean Carly's father?"

"Also known as Mayor Vance," Chance bites out. "You

think I'm the only one with issues about you having your hand in Carly's panties?"

And on her perfect tits at the spring.

I glance at Miles. I've only known my middle brother for a few days, but I recognize that look on his face. It mirrors my own.

This has got *oh shit* written all over it.

 ARLY

My nerves are jumping under my skin, and all I've done so far is sit down on one of the sticky vinyl booth seats at Millie's. I'm wearing jeans, as I just came from Bridger Ranch. I left a little early so I can get this over with during one of the restaurant's lulls and be home for dinner, my mother none the wiser. She'd want to come with me, to literally hold my hand, but this is something I have to do on my own.

I recall how my bare thighs used to stick to these seats.

I was wearing shorts that last day...

No!

I steel myself and glance at the plastic-coated menu, complete with vintage photographs of the selections.

It hasn't changed in five years. The vanilla malt is still a sickly yellow color, and the kid's menu still includes the famous wiener man—a hot dog sliced lengthwise halfway and then boiled so the two halves look like legs, topped off with mustard eyeballs and a ketchup smile. I used to gobble it up as a kid. Now it looks kind of disgusting.

I stare out the smudged window at the town before me. Luna is dusting in the window of her antique shop, and Branson's barber pole is spinning already. Small town life. Everything opens early but the town shuts down by six. Except for Millie's and the Mexican restaurant, Las Casas. They stay open for the dinner crowd.

A waitress wearing a standard pink uniform cracks her gum beside my booth. "What'll it be, sweetie?" Then she gets an eyeful. "Oh! Hello there, Carly."

My cheeks warm, but I'm determined not to feel embarrassed. This is just a diner. A run-of-the-mill diner in a run-of-the-mill small town. Sure, it took me more than two days to follow through on the determination I had with Dr. Lake to get here. But I'm here now.

"Hi, Emma," I say. "Is Millie here?"

"She's off today." Emma gives me that eye-softening look full of pity. "How have you been?"

"Just fine, thanks." I don't mean to be short with her,

but I'm here for a reason. To check this visit off my damned list. "I'll have the grilled cheese with bacon, please. And black coffee."

"Coming right up." Emma whisks away, tears the sheet off her pad, and hangs it on the round thing where the cook will grab it.

She means well.

They all mean well.

But I'm so over it. I think it was my parents who were so dead set against me getting a job that gave me the first hard push. Then Chance punching Austin for making out with poor Carly. Then it was Austin himself—not in a bad way, but a good one—that has me ready to move on completely. To leave the shackles truly in the past.

My nerves have settled a little. This isn't the booth I sat in *that* day. I tried. I really did when I came in the door. But I couldn't, and Dr. Lake didn't make it a requirement.

Emma drops off a cup of steaming coffee, and I take a cautious sip. It tastes like brown water, but Millie's coffee always has. I don't pull out my phone, only look out the window as I focus on my breathing, on seeing the town through the window. A few minutes later, Emma returns with my sandwich and a side of hash browns I didn't ask for. Except they're not hash browns. They're tater tots with seasoned salt. But Millie has always called them hash browns.

And why am I ruminating on hash browns? Who the hell cares? I'm not going to eat them anyway. I'm not even slightly hungry, but eating isn't what this visit is about.

I place the paper napkin across my lap and take another sip of the flavorless coffee.

And though I try not to…I remember.

Five years ago, during spring break of my first year of veterinary school, I was eating here at the diner with my friend Ashley and I excused myself to go to the bathroom. The one off the back hallway.

I never returned. Until now.

For a long time, I couldn't remember what happened. All I knew was that I woke up in some kind of maze running for my life. That lasted a few days, and then another memory jump…and I was on the island. I can feel the heat on my face. The humidity. Breathe in the tang of the sea air.

Again, running for my life. But you can only run so long before you get caught.

Through some guided hypnosis with Dr. Lake, I recalled getting jumped in the bathroom stall, and then the prick of a needle in my neck. I never saw the face of my attacker, and no one seemed to witness the assault or see me get taken out the back way of the diner.

From Bayfield, Montana. The place where nothing happens to anyone. Except me.

So much is still a mystery—who took me and how I got to the island—but at least Derek Wolfe is dead and his kids shut down his vicious trafficking enterprise. Most of the men who went there are either in prison or have disappeared—having fled the country. It's over.

No reason to fear for my life here. Not today. Objectively, I know this.

I draw in a deep breath. The smoky fragrance of the bacon wafts into me, and my stomach actually growls a little. I've always loved bacon.

Maybe I will take a bite of my sandwich, but first...

I have to go to the ladies room.

I have to face the place where I was abducted.

That's the main reason for coming back to Millie's.

*You have to know that you're safe there, Car*ly, Dr. Lake says.

But I wasn't safe there.

Not then. But you are now.

I stand.

Emma hurries over, worry etched on her aged face. "Do you need something?"

"Just going to pee, Emma," I say.

"Oh." Her cheeks redden. "Sorry."

Yes, it would be nice to be able to do so without the entire diner feeling like I may vanish if they don't keep their eyes trained on me at all times.

I walk slowly, my heart rattling in my chest, toward the ladies' room near the back of the diner.

The back door.

The door I was carried out of.

It looms in the distance, not seeming to get any nearer until I almost run into it.

To my right is the door to the bathroom.

I turn and push it open.

The pungent scent of fruity air freshener assaults me. It's a small bathroom with only two stalls. I was in the second one when...

I draw in another breath to calm my racing heart and push the door to the stall open—

"Hey!" A woman inside slams the door closed.

I jump, panicked and embarrassed at the same time.

"Oh God! I'm sorry."

"Didn't you see my legs?"

"I...wasn't looking. Why didn't you lock the door?"

"The lock doesn't work."

"God. I'm so sorry." I wash my hands quickly, leave the bathroom, and head back to my table, glancing out the front picture windows. Sweat dots my brow and I'm glad I didn't eat any of my sandwich because I'm instantly nauseated.

God. Even more so when I see my father walking down the sidewalk.

He doesn't look happy. In fact, he looks downright pissed.

Coming toward him?

The three Bridger brothers.

Uh-oh.

Based on the not-so fun conversation over dinner the other night, I can't forget that Dad hates them. Because the elder—and dead—Bridger swindled him out of his property. Fair enough. I lost three years of my life. I know what being robbed feels like.

But the faceoff between the Bridger brothers and my dad is a surefire recipe for disaster.

I love my dad, but I also love my job. I *need* my job. If Chance ends up firing me because of a blowup with my dad...

I've felt more whole in the last few days than I've felt in five years.

Why can't Dad understand that?

Why can't he see that Austin, Miles, and Chance aren't their father?

I look to Austin and feel a catch in my chest. There's something about him that works for me. All three Bridger brothers are handsome, but it's Austin who melts my butter. And wets my panties.

I head to my table, grab my wallet out of my purse,

and throw some bills on the table to cover my uneaten sandwich.

Then I draw in a deep breath. I need to get between the men because I'm definitely the center of their upcoming fight. I can feel it.

I know it.

I dash out of the restaurant, the little bell clanging over the door as I go.

This won't be pretty.

13

USTIN

RICK VANCE IS TALL, about my height, and doesn't look any happier to see us up close. He stops, blocking the sidewalk, clearly ready for a chat.

Or a Wild West shootout.

He doesn't seem to be sporting a gun on his hip, but this is Montana.

I see bits of Carly in him—the dark hair and coloring, although his eyes are a deep brown instead of a vibrant green.

I glance at Miles, who gives away nothing, since he's about as clueless as I am. The best thing is to follow

Chance's lead when it comes to this guy and keep my mouth shut about having my hands on his daughter.

"Mayor." Chance tips his Stetson. His stance is wide as he tucks his thumbs in his jeans pockets.

"Bridger." The mayor doesn't crack a smile, only narrows his gaze and glowers. "I'm glad I ran into you. It'll save me a trip to your place."

His tone indicates he isn't going to stop by to watch sports and drink beers.

"Oh? What can I do for you?" Chance prods cautiously. "I already made a sizable donation to the renovation fund for the library."

Man, does Chance hate everyone? Pretty much all Miles and I've seen is gruff. Grumpy. Angry. I don't remember seeing Chance crack a smile, even when telling something he's philanthropic.

Mayor Vance cocks his head, and is that a sly smile splitting his lips?

"It has come to light that the dam you have on Shipp's Creek is impacting the water rights of those downstream."

Chance takes off his Stetson, runs his hand over his head, and then sets it back on. "That's interesting and all since the Bridgers have the oldest water rights in the state."

Seattle has rain. A shit ton of it. Water isn't an issue. To me, it's what I land my plane on and get when I turn on a faucet. I'm not familiar with the ins and outs of what the hell they're talking about.

"Still can't prevent others from getting enough to water their crops." The older man puffs up his chest, clearly pleased with his argument.

"Right. That *dam*, as you call it, is a bunch of rocks and tree branches. Beavers create more water blockage than anything on my property ever could. I have no interest or intention of creating a problem for any of my neighbors."

"*Our* property," Miles murmurs.

Chance turns his head and gives Miles a wry look. "*Ours*," he corrects. "Mr. Mayor, have you met the *other* Bridgers? This is Austin and Miles."

The man's eyes widen as he takes us in without taking the hands we both offer. "What?" he asks roughly, as if he's swallowed his own spit.

A smile slowly spreads across Chance's face. Yeah, finally. A fucking smile.

"Oh, you didn't hear? You seem to have your finger on the pulse of everything in this community. Including my"—he clears his throat—"*our* father. Except he no longer has a pulse."

I swear I can see Rick Vance's back molars grinding together.

"There are three of you? Jesus." He runs a hand over his face.

I have a feeling we're not going to get a town-sanctioned welcoming parade.

"That's right." Chance nods. "Not just me you have to deal with now."

I have to remember he's Carly's dad. *Carly's dad.*

"I'm sure I can ring up my lawyer and have him look into any water rights issues you might have," Chance continues, his voice steady. "Or I can ride downstream and chat with my neighbors personally about the pesky wildlife. Or I can move a few rocks and alleviate the problem personally." Chance holds his arm out, indicating me and Miles. "I've got some strong backs to help me."

"Moving a few rocks won't solve the issues I have with the Bridgers," Mr. Vance growls.

"I'm well aware of that, since you always seem to have one or two." Chance takes a step toward the older man. "Please stop by and share any additional issues you may have, but just a reminder, Mayor. I'm not my father."

"You sure about that?" Mr. Vance narrows his gaze even further until his eyes are practically slits. His face is getting redder by the minute. "Your old man threw money around like it fixed everything. What happens when that money goes away? Huh?"

"Dad!"

Chance, Miles, and I turn as one at the female voice.

Carly's rushing down the sidewalk toward us, her eyes wide with concern. The last time I saw her, she was mostly naked and I was cupping her perfect tits after bringing her to orgasm. I start to get hard at the thought, which is a big fucking problem.

She gives the three of us a quick glance and then moves to her dad. She goes on tiptoes and kisses his cheek. That helps my dick go down, even though she looks damned hot in a snug pair of jeans and a sleeveless blouse with little ruffles at the shoulders. Her hair's back in a braid and not a lick of makeup on her pretty face. Concern mars her smooth brow...

And she went to her dad and not me.

I scratch my jaw where I longed for her lips to brush.

Two men stand here who, if they knew, would be really unhappy that I have plans for Carly—plans that involve her naked and beneath me. Her dad hates the Bridgers—including me because of my damned last name. I haven't even said a word and I'm the enemy. It's not going to get any better either.

"What's going on?" Carly asks.

"Just having a little chat with the Bridger boys, sweetheart."

She looks at each of us but settles her gaze on me. "About what?"

"Nothing a little chat with some beavers won't solve." Chance's voice is tempered. For her.

His look is kind and gentle when he turns it Carly's way. Obviously, he still doesn't want to upset the woman, even if her dad is being a dick. Perhaps *especially* because of that.

"Beavers?" Carly cocks her head, frowning. "You're not expected to deal with them on our... I mean, *their* land, are you? They can be mean—the beavers, not the Bridgers—and since they own—"

"What the—?" Chance cuts himself off. "What do you mean, Carly? *They own* what?"

"Your dad bought our land and we're renting it back," she replies. "Or rather, the city is renting the house for us."

Chance frowns. "Jonathan bought your property? When the he— heck did this happen?"

Vance huffs. "Like you didn't know."

"Are you crazy?" Chance shakes his head. "You think my old man let me in on any of his dealings? Or that he didn't leave us in a bind when he up and died?"

"Right," Vance says.

Chance holds his hands up. "Whatever, Mayor. Think what you want. I don't give a shit. I'm not airing the Bridger dirty laundry with you."

I don't blame Chance for shutting down. The mayor

isn't receptive to anything he has to say and at least Chance will walk away with his pride.

"A big-ass bind," Miles offers.

"I don't give a rat's ass what kind of *bind* he left you in," Mayor Vance says. "I've been researching your father since I was elected and he skirted the law for the last couple decades. What he did with our land is only one shady deal."

"That's our father, not us," I say.

I feel oddly protective of my brother. Why? I have no idea. He's a grumpy asshole that put Miles and me on a chain gang work program. But what I know of Chance, he's got honor that our dad never had.

"I'd say throw the guy in jail," Miles says, "but oh yeah, he's dead. Talk about a bind."

"Chance," Carly says, "just sell my father his land back. Or pay him what it's worth. You've got the money."

As if it's that simple. Which it is when billions of dollars can solve lots of problems. Including this one. Except we can't get the money.

"Carly." Vance sets his hand on her shoulder. "This isn't a problem for you to worry about."

"But—"

"Wait, wait, wait." Chance rubs his jaw. "Our father didn't *pay* you?"

"It's not that simple." Vance looks at Carly. "The

Bridgers have been paying everyone off to get their way for years, and I for one am sick of it. You people are not above the law. I don't care how much money you've got socked away."

"Mayor, I'm happy to right my father's wrong," Chance says. "I'll talk to our lawyer and I'll see if something can be arranged."

"See, Daddy?" Carly smiles. Sort of. "You'll get your ranch back and you won't have to be mayor any more to make ends meet. You can go back to working your land, which I know you loved doing. Mom can get her hens back, and we can have fresh eggs, and—"

"Dude," Miles interrupts, looking at Chance. "We can't get at any of the money for a year. Remember what Sharple said."

"You mean Shankle," I correct.

"Whatever." Miles rolls his eyes. "The guy might be an odd duck and probably sleeps with his briefcase, but he's got the three of us by the balls. He was pretty clear."

"Surely we can get enough out of the ranch trust to pay off the Vances," Chance says. "Can you tell me exactly what happened, Mayor?"

"Why don't you check your own damned records, Bridger? You'll find a hell of a lot more than one bad land deal." Vance turns. "Let's go, Carly."

"Daddy," Carly pleads. "Please. At least sit down with

them and talk this out. Talk to their attorney. Maybe we can—"

"We can't." Vance eyes his daughter.

Carly looks to me, to her father, to me again.

Does she want me to say something that can help? I can't. I won't out our relationship—if you can even call it that—here in the middle of town. In front of her father, who already despises me. It's new. And different. Potent, because no matter how much I think I should stay away from her, no matter how clear Chance was about me leaving her alone, I can't.

When she stripped down and waded into the spring with me, set my hands on her tits to lavish on, she became mine. There's so much shit in our way, unbelievable baggage. I don't want to add to it.

And I don't want to get punched in the face again, this time on Main Street.

I don't think Carly wants me to give the thing between us away, but clearly she's hoping I'll do something.

But what?

Damn it all. Now she's pleading with those fucking green eyes. Pleading with me to fix this, and I want to fix it for her.

I want to fix everything for her.

But I don't know what to do. What to say. I know nothing about the Bridger business, only that it's worth billions. I open my mouth, thinking I'll agree with Chance, that somehow we'll pay Vance what he's owed, but then I close it.

Because I don't know if we can. I'm helpless all over again, just like when we learned about my mother's disease. How it's not fixable.

I can't take away the horrors of Carly's past. I can't take away what Jonathan Bridger did to Chance, Miles, me, and countless others. My hands are fucking tied and I hate it.

I just don't know shit, and I won't make a promise to Carly that I'm not sure I can keep. God, I feel so damned useless. I'm letting her down, and that's the last thing I want.

Her pretty smile morphs into a straight line, and her gaze falls on the sidewalk.

She steps toward her father. "Let's go, Daddy."

"Good call." Vance glares at the three of us. "Carly won't be back at work tomorrow. Or ever again."

Carly gasps. "That's not what I meant. I—"

"It's for the best, little one." Mayor Vance gently takes her arm. "Let's go."

I watch Carly walk away, and with each step, she takes another piece of my heart. Because a curvy slip of a woman has penetrated every one of my defenses.

I turn to Chance, my temper on fire. "Fix this. You have to fix this shit."

"You heard the man." Chance takes off his Stetson and slaps it on his jean-clad thigh. "He doesn't want our money. Damn. He wants our hides."

"Just exactly what kind of a man was Jonathan Bridger?" Miles asks. "Because while I knew he was an asshole, a lot of other people think the same thing."

"He was a dick," Chance says, "but the two of you already know that. Vance, too. He didn't win any popularity contests in town, but I never thought he was a damned criminal."

"Vance didn't call him a criminal," I clarify, glancing in the direction Carly went. They've turned a corner and are out of sight.

"Not outright, he didn't." Chance adjusts his hat back on his head. "But he said our father was skirting the law for years, which doesn't sound off brand for him. Or that he cheated the Vance family out of their property."

"That's some great genetic material we've got," I say, more to myself than to my brothers. Then I realize that Chance *knew* the guy. Maybe better than anyone else. "What *aren't* you telling us?"

He pulls a red bandana out of his pocket and rubs the sweat off his forehead. "You know what I know."

"You lived with the guy," Miles prompts.

Chance rolls his eyes. "You're in the house, and you know how big it is. Shit, you could have a threesome in your room and I'd never see the women come in the house or hear a thing."

Miles grins. "Good to know."

It's my turn to roll my eyes. "You can't tell me you never had dinner together? Passed in the hall? Hell, saw each other while working? He didn't mention he took the Vance land?"

"To him, I was an employee, just like everyone else on the ranch. The only difference is I lived in the house. You asked about facts. I don't know shit about what Vance mentioned or the deal itself. I mean, there have been rumors for years, but my father always told me to pay them no mind. That the townsfolk were just jealous."

It's easy to be jealous of billions of dollars.

"Uh...what kind of rumors?" Anger slithers up my spine. The more I learn about Jonathan Bridger, the more I hate him.

If my bastard father hurt Carly's family, after everything they've already been through...

Vance may be angry, but he seems justified, although his focus is directed at the wrong people. Still...

"We've got to find a way to fix this," I say, this time to both my brothers.

"I agree," Miles says. "I know the mayor came on

pretty strong, but I don't get the feeling that he's a bad guy."

Yeah, he's thinking like me.

"Then he ought to know we aren't our father," Chance says. "But he doesn't seem to."

I rub at my temples, which are starting to ache. "Let's just make a deal with Vance. In a year, when we get our money, we'll pay him the fair market value of his property plus a healthy amount of interest. Surely he'll agree to that."

Except I don't believe my words.

Rick Vance might want his land back, but his focus now doesn't seem to be the Bridger money.

He seems out for Bridger blood. That means mine. I knew it was tainted all along, but now it's truly fucking with me. Vance's hatred is like a sticky web, ensnaring Carly in it. Making her unhappy, which I don't like at all.

Miles and I sit in the truck when Chance runs into the store for the supplies he needs and then we mutually decide to ditch the beer idea. We don't talk much during the drive back to the ranch. I spend the time ruminating on how I disappointed Carly and how I can make it up to her.

I come up with zilch. I can't fix my mom being sick. I don't know how to fix this because I have no clue what's going on.

Fuck.

We pull into the long driveway only to see a black Jaguar parked off in one of the guest spots.

"Shankle," Chance says. "Is he going to check up on us all year long?"

"I don't give a shit about that." I click open the door of the truck. "But we can ask him about Vance's land. See if we have enough money available to pay him off. I'll forgo part of my thousand dollars a month if I have to."

"That won't be enough, Austin," Miles says. "I'm not an expert on ranch land in Montana, but I know real estate."

I sigh. I knew that when I said it. But damn, I'm willing to try anything. Anything to bring that beautiful smile back to Carly's face. Anything to ease the ache in my gut from disappointing her. Because if Vance gets his way, she's not coming back to work. Yeah, it would suck if I didn't see her here, but this is about her happiness. I know how much she loves her job.

"Fine. But there's one way to find out," Chance says.

We walk into the house, give the dogs a few belly rubs, and then head into the living room where Shankle is sitting. In his black suit, bolo tie, and felt hat, he looks a lot like Johnny Cash. Funny I didn't notice the resemblance the first couple times I met him.

"Mr. Shankle," Chance says. "Didn't realize we were out past curfew."

"Boys," he says, ignoring Chance's sarcasm, "we've got a problem."

Great. A problem. As if the list of problems isn't long enough already.

Just great.

14

ARLY

I HAVE no intention of leaving my job at Bridger Ranch, but telling that to my father now isn't a good idea.

I want information from him.

"Daddy," I say, when we get to the old brick building that doubles as city hall and the courthouse, "please tell me. What has Jonathan Bridger done?"

He opens the entry door without responding. It's late in the afternoon and the building is quiet. There aren't many court cases, but unless it's something big—which never happens in Bayfield to anyone but me—they're wrapped up in the mornings.

"Good morning, Mayor, Carly." The bright-eyed receptionist smiles when we walk in.

"Doris." Dad nods and heads straight to his office at the end of the hallway.

I simply wave and close the door to his office, taking a seat in front of his desk. He's already settled behind it, tapping on his computer keyboard.

"Daddy..."

"In a minute, Carly. I need to take care of a few things." He continues tapping.

I look around the tiny office's beige walls, a metal desk, and a few faded photos of the Montana Big Sky country on the walls. It's not much, but Bayfield is a small town. The sign as you enter says *Welcome to Bayfield. Don't blink or you'll miss it.*

In reality, it's a little bigger than that. Population of the city proper is about five thousand, but as mayor, Dad is also the chairman of the board of county commissioners, so he has jurisdiction over all the land that surrounds the town—including Bridger Ranch.

Dad hits return and then turns to me, setting his forearms on his desk and folding his hands. Gone is the angry glare he shared with the Bridgers.

"Your mother doesn't want you working, but I'll allow it. I'm going to help you find another position. I've been looking since you announced your new job, and I've got a couple possibilities."

"No, Dad. I don't want to talk about that." No way in hell am I sitting beside Doris and stuffing envelopes. "I want to talk about the Bridgers, and not with regard to my job."

"The Bridgers aren't your concern," he counters.

If he only knew...

I'm all but in love with one of them. Seeing Austin on the street with his brothers—arguing with my dad—made me realize I wanted to leave with him, not my father. I wanted to take his hand and run. To escape to our secret spring where it's just the two of us. No problems. No outside world.

"I've known Chance for a long time," I say. "I've told you before that he's a good guy."

Dad swipes his hand through the air. "Good guy? How could he be with Jonathan Bridger as his father? Now there are two more of them. They're ruthless, sweetheart, and I don't want you near any of them. You no longer work for them."

My spine stiffens at his cut-and-dried decision making when it comes to my life. My friends. My...lover.

I *do* work at Bridger Ranch and I'll continue as long as I wish. My father doesn't own me. I've spent enough time with men having power over me, and I'm done. Of course, unlike the others in the past, he means well, but that somehow makes it worse.

I feel smothered. Suffocated instead of free.

If Dad knew about what I've already done and shared with Austin, he'd probably have a stroke. He'd probably even try to ground me like I was sixteen. I might be his daughter, but I'm not his little girl any longer. I can decide for myself who's good and who's bad. I've certainly had enough experience with that.

I let out a sigh and try to get through to him one more time. I don't want to choose, but I might have to. "Just tell me, Dad. What did their father do, other than pay you less than what your property was worth?"

His dark eyes flick to mine. "You won't understand."

"Seriously?" I shake my head. "Last time I checked I was a college graduate and I got into vet school, which is highly selective. You saw my test scores. Don't patronize me like that."

His gaze softens. "You're an intelligent gi—"

I glare at him.

He clears his throat. "Young woman."

"I'm twenty-seven years old. You were married and had me by that age," I remind him.

"You're still healing. This isn't something you need to

concern yourself with. And the Bridgers—the ranch and the men—are bad for you."

I groan. I know bad men much better than my father does. "Jesus, Dad. What if I want to get involved in what you're accusing them of? To know what's going on with my own family, with my employers?" *With Austin.* "Can't I make my own opinions?" *With Austin.*

He wrinkles his forehead. "Why would you want to get into the mess? You need calm, not stress. I'm going to find you another position without any complications. The Bridgers don't need to be part of your life."

Like Austin Bridger—who stood there like a statue, eyeing me with the same confusion I felt. The same need.

What did I expect from Austin during that confrontation? He never even knew his father. He couldn't say anything. Did he even have anything to share? He told me he'd never met his dad before, never been to the ranch before last week and that he's only here now because of the will. Because Jonathan Bridger bequeathed it.

I bite my lower lip, thinking back. I wasn't fair, pleading with my eyes at him the way I did. There was nothing he could do. If he had spoken up, what would he have said? Or done? If he acknowledged knowing me, even in passing on the ranch, he might have given us away. Chance would be pissed. My dad would be more than pissed.

I don't want to be a dirty secret, but I also don't want to be told what to do. Who to see. Who to care for.

"All right, sweetheart. We'll talk, but later. The monthly city council meeting is tonight and I have to prepare."

"Tomorrow morning then?"

"Yes," he relents, his shoulder relaxing. "At breakfast."

It will have to do. In the meantime, I have someone else to deal with. Someone who makes my heart race and my pussy clench. The last time I talked to Austin, he had his hands on my breasts. I want that again, and more.

Because the one thing I've been sure about lately is Austin. And me. And while I know what's happening between us was fast, that I barely know him, I'm not letting fear stop me. The one orgasm he gave me was like a drug. I want more. Need it.

Crave it.

And that was his fingers. I ache for what he could do with his mouth and his dick. I'm finding satisfaction from a man, just as Dr. Lake suggested.

For the first time in ages, I want something. And I'm going to get it. Doctor sanctioned, too.

I rise, lean forward across his desk, and give him a quick kiss on his cheek. "Thanks, Daddy."

I leave his office, stride down the hallway, say a quick goodbye to Doris, and exit the building.

I'm going to go to Bridger Ranch, and not to work. I want something.

Dick.

I want it and the only one who can give it to me is Austin—a family enemy.

15

USTIN

"Have a seat," Shankle says.

Interesting. It's our huge-ass house, and he's telling *us* to have a seat.

But Chance obeys him as if the lawyer has him under some kind of thrall.

Miles and I look at each other. He shrugs. I shrug back.

Then we both drop onto the couch facing Shankle. He props his foot up on his knee, relaxed as usual.

"I'm glad you're here," Chance says. "We need to have a piece of property appraised and then pay Rick Vance the difference between the fair market value and what my father paid him for it."

"Who the hell is Rick Vance?" Shankle asks.

"The mayor of Bayfield."

He pauses a moment and then shakes his head. "Right. Well, I'm afraid that's not going to happen."

"We know we can't get our money for a year," I say, "but can't we make an exception? The mayor thinks our esteemed father screwed him over, and from the little I know about the asshole, he probably has a case."

"Rick Vance—hell, the entire city of Bayfield—is the least of your problems right now." Shankle adjusts his bolo, loosening it as if he's choking.

"What's going on?" Miles asks.

"I got a phone call from a source at the DOJ this morning."

"The Department of Justice?" Miles's eyes widen.

Shankle nods and then clears his throat so gruffly I'm convinced he's going to hock a hunk of phlegm right onto the marble coffee table.

"And...?" Miles prods.

Another throat clear. "Apparently your father's death has put some...things in motion."

"I'm almost afraid to ask," I say on a groan.

"Apparently, as long as he was alive," Shankle continues, "there were certain fail-safes in place. But his death triggered the release of some information that would have been better left buried."

"For Christ's sake," Chance says. "Just what are you getting at?"

"The DOJ has probable cause to believe that your father was involved in some criminal activity, and they're petitioning to have all of the Bridger assets frozen."

I drop my jaw.

Miles drops his jaw.

Chance drops his jaw. "You're kidding, right?"

Shankle leans in and aims his gaze at Chance. "Would I have come out here unannounced if I were kidding?"

"Exactly what type of criminal activity was he involved in?" Miles asks.

"*Allegedly* involved in," I remind him, not that I'm on the dead guy's side. I've tried and found my sperm donor guilty in my head. Too bad he's dead and can't rot in a prison cell for all the shit he seems to have done.

Shankle coughs into his hand, this time sounding like he's about to choke up a lung.

"You need to lay off the smokes," Chance says.

Shankle ignores him. "I assume at least you, Chance, know that your father had other investments outside the ranch."

"Sure," Chance says casually.

"First, let me assure you that all the money generated

from the Bridger Ranch is clean. I made sure your father's personal funds were never commingled with that of the family land."

An anvil settles in my gut. I've got a real bad feeling about what's coming.

"Just spit it out." Miles rakes his fingers through his blond locks.

"Bridger Investments has majority holdings in many chemical plants throughout the US and Canada. The DOJ says they have evidence that several of the plants here in the states have been illegally disposing of hazardous materials in direct violation of EPA regulations. If these allegations are proved..."

"Just say it," Chance says.

"There are criminal penalties." Shankle coughs again.

"You mean prison time?" I ask, completely astounded. What the fuck have I walked into?

"Yes, but since you and Miles have had nothing to do with your father's business, it won't affect either of you."

"Hey"—Chance rises, his gaze landing on Shankle—"I knew—*know*—nothing about my father's other holdings. He shared nothing with me. Nothing."

"And you never asked?" Shankle says.

"The few times I did, he told me to mind my own fucking business. I'm a rancher. That's it. I had nothing to do with anything else."

"It'll be a harder sell since you lived and worked beside him." Shankle adjusts his bolo. "But we can probably prove you knew nothing."

I regard my youngest half brother. His fair complexion has gone even paler. He's scared, and pissed based on the way his jaw is clenched. For good reason. Chance has been a pain in my ass, but the man's not a criminal.

"That'll keep you out of the slammer," Shankle continues, "but that's not the only criminal penalty you might get. There are hefty fines. Plus you three will be ordered to clean up your mess."

"*Our* mess?" This time I stand. "We didn't have anything to do with this."

"No, but your father did, and someone has to take responsibility in civil court. You're his heirs."

Right. The billion fucking heirs.

"For fuck's sake." I shake my head.

"Look, nothing's been proven yet, but they clearly have evidence, otherwise they wouldn't be threatening to freeze the assets."

"Something is off about this." Chance stands and paces behind the oversized leather couch. "My father may have been a first-class bastard, but he wasn't stupid. If he had a fail-safe in place, he would have made arrangements for an untimely demise."

"Yeah, he had enough time to create his ironclad will

that's got me sitting here instead of getting bagels at a shop on Fifty-Eighth Street," Miles says.

"Would he have though?" I ask. "He died suddenly, right? Of an aneurysm?"

Shankle nods. "Yeah, and it was unexpected. Chance can tell you that Jonathan was lean and mean. The chance of an aneurysm, even at his age of fifty-eight, was slim to none, especially with no family history."

"So where is this investigation coming from?" I demand. "Some whistleblower he paid to keep quiet?"

"Give the boy a silver dollar." Shankle smiles.

If he calls me *boy* one more time...

But I've got worse shit to deal with.

"Fine, he freezes the assets," Miles says. "Austin and I aren't expecting a dime until next summer. But how the hell do we run this business—the ranch—if we can't get at any money?"

"There's overhead, Shankle," Chance says. "Payroll. Running a ranch of this size isn't cheap. Hell, you're not sitting here for free, I'm sure."

"I've got the top environmental partner at my firm looking into this," Shankle replies, skimming over the fact that he's probably clearing a pretty penny due to this new development. "Plus a guy with white-collar criminal experience. With my financial savvy, we can probably get the Feds to agree to keep funding available for day-to-day business operations of the ranch. Plus, nothing has happened yet."

Yet. He wouldn't be here if he didn't think *yet* might be coming soon.

"This is fucked." I sit back down on the couch and turn to Miles. "You and I may as well go home. So much for our billions."

"If you leave, you forfeit everything," Shankle reminds us. "Nothing has been proven yet."

"Except that Jonathan Bridger is officially an asshole," I say.

"Truth, but Jesus Fucking Christ," Miles mutters. "This is a mess."

"Did you know anything about this, Shankle?" I demand.

He shakes his head. "I'm Bridger's estate attorney and his general counsel with regard to the ranch. Once the year is up and you've met the requirements of the will, my service to your father is done. Regardless, I have nothing to do with his outside holdings, nor do I know who handles them. If the DOJ is involved, it's got to be expansive."

"So no attorney-client privilege, then." From Miles. "Of course, he's dead anyway."

"Attorney-client privilege survives the death of the client," Shankle clarifies. "But it doesn't apply here for two reasons. First, this is all news to me, so there's no privilege. And second, a client's communication to his attorney isn't privileged if he made it with the intention of committing or covering up a crime or fraud."

Chance plunks his ass back down on his chair. "We are so fucked."

"We?" Miles lifts his eyebrows. "He kept me and Austin out of his life completely."

"Until now when he's dead. Until this shit comes up," Chance reminds us.

"Boys…" Shankle begins.

I stand again, this time lunging over the marble coffee table and pulling Shankle up by his bolo-tied collar. "I swear to God, if you call us boys one more time—"

"Easy." Miles stands and jerks me backward. "This doesn't have anything to do with the two of us."

"Yes, it fucking does!" I release Shankle and throw him back down on the couch.

I spin, running my hand over the back of my neck.

"We can't walk away from this cluster fuck," I tell my brothers. "I need that money. I have a dying seaplane business and a sick mother. I have no choice but to stay and be sucked into this shit."

I walk out of the living room, out of the damned house, knowing the problems will follow.

 ARLY

I'M CRAZY. *Crazy.*

I shift once again beneath the cool sheets, second guessing every bit of confidence I lumped together to get here. I had a plan. To show up at Bridger Ranch, sneak into Austin's room and seduce him.

The only thing that went right was that I parked by the stable as I usually did without incident. Then things fell apart a bit.

I ran into Lexie, who was late leaving for the day, and I had to lie and tell her I forgot my phone. She left after I pretended to go into the staff room to grab my not-left-behind cell. When she was gone, I sneaked up to the main house, hoping to slip in through the back door and to Austin's room. The plan was to have him asleep, naked, and I'd climb in and we'd have sex.

However Miles caught me barely inside the house. I was tiptoeing across the kitchen, my work boots grasped between my fingers. I was so nervous just sneaking in that my heart rate was out of control. When Miles closed the fridge door and grinned at me, I felt like a deer caught in the middle of the road before being plowed down by a cement truck.

———

"HEY THERE," Miles says, holding a beer. Of the three brothers, he's the quietest. But the wildest, I think. He's rough around the edges, just like I imagine most from New York.

I glance at the back door, wishing I could just disappear. And he could forget he ever saw me. Then I whip my head around, hoping Chance isn't here. Or Austin, because I'll have to do some serious lying as to why I've entered their house unannounced and uninvited.

I'm here to have sex with Austin. To use him for orgasms and hope his dick is as talented as his fingers.

"Hi," I whisper, my voice catching in my throat. "Um..."

"You're here for Austin."

I nod, swallowing hard.

"He's not here."

I slump my shoulders, feeling defeated.

"Neither is Chance, so take a breath."

I do exactly that, but I'm not all that relieved. "I suck at seduction."

My hands fly to my mouth. No, I didn't. I did not just tell Miles Bridger that I suck at seduction.

He laughs and rakes his gaze over me. From any other guy, it might seem creepy, but Miles seems to be assessing and thinking—not undressing me with his eyes.

Well, maybe a little.

"I can see why Austin's all in with you."

"Oh?" I ask, lost.

"You've already seduced the man and you don't even know it."

I huff. "Except he's not here and we're not—"

"Fucking?"

My cheeks heat.

"Yet. But I'm guessing that's the plan, and why you're headed for his room?"

I nod.

And hope a hole opens up in the floor to swallow me and put this embarrassing situation out of its misery.

"Down that hall." He points. "Last door on the left."

He's not steering me away. Or poking fun. Or telling me I shouldn't go through with it.

He's not shaming me.

He's helping.

I blink at him. "Um...thanks?"

"You're welcome. Have fun."

God, could I be any more mortified?

Maybe I should go. This was a stupid idea. What was I thinking? I turn toward the door, ready to tuck my proverbial tail between my legs and go home. To my childhood bedroom. And my vibrator.

"Don't you dare chicken out now, Carly. You've made it this far."

I stop and realize he's right.

I nod and spin around again, heading toward Austin's room.

"Hey, Carly?"

I glance at him over my shoulder.

"If you can't tell, this place is huge. No one'll hear you if you're a little loud."

He winks and I scurry off.

———

For thirty minutes I've been lying naked between Austin's cool sheets, and second thoughts are invading my mind. Again. I'm in the middle of a nervous spiral of doubt when I hear footfall coming down the hallway.

I swallow and tug the sheet over me.

The door opens, and in strides Austin.

He looks like a god. His hair is windblown, and his cheeks are shiny with sweat. What this man can do to a plain white T-shirt...

He stops short when he sees me, his hand still on the door.

"Holy fuck," he breathes, raking his gaze over me.

He stares. I stare back.

He stares some more.

I squirm. "Hi."

"What are you doing here?" He kicks the door shut with his foot, his eyes never leaving mine.

I frown. "If you can't tell, I'm not doing it right."

"Oh, you're sure as hell doing it right, but why? I thought we were going to take this slow."

I sit up, tugging the sheet with me.

"Jesus, you're naked, aren't you?"

I am. I might have a vibrator, but I don't have sexy underwear. Even having never done this before, I know plain cotton panties and bras aren't part of any seduction routine.

His words rile me. Not the naked part, but before that.

"*You* thought, Austin. *You* thought we were going to

take this slow. I wanted it at the spring. I want it now. I really want to finish what we started at the Dusty Rose. I want more orgasms. I want sex. I'm ready for it. I *ache* for it."

His brow wings up and a slow smile spreads across his face. "You ache, sweetheart?"

I nod and my cheeks warm at all I just admitted. I do. I *so* ache for him, and my tone only helps give me away. I'm wet and my clit throbs with need. He hasn't thrown me out. In fact, he's toeing off his boots as he reaches behind his neck to tug off his T-shirt. I saw him at the spring in only his boxer briefs, but seeing his chest again makes my mouth water.

His shoulders are broad, his waist narrow. Muscles bulge and flex as he takes off his clothes. I remembered how he felt beneath my hands, but hopefully now I'll have time to explore.

"I'm sorry about earlier," he says. "In town."

He opens his belt buckle.

"I didn't know what to say to your dad because I didn't—"

"I don't think now's the time to talk about my father."

He pushes his jeans and boxers down and off and he stands upright, his dick—hard and thick and long—bobbing upward against his belly.

Yeah, I don't want to talk about my father at all. Austin is more amazing than I imagined.

He moves to the side of the bed. "Drop the sheet."

I swallow again, my nerves skittering.

He grips the base of his dick and squeezes. With a tight fist, he strokes himself from root to tip and a bead of liquid oozes from the slit. "This is what you do to me, Carly. I love that you're here. That you want to do this with me."

He reaches out and curls his fingers into the sheet that's hiked between my breasts. The hold has the fabric lowering a little, although if I truly wanted to stay covered, I could resist.

But it's futile now.

He's here.

He's what I want.

I won't let a piece of cloth get in the way now.

I drop my hands to my sides so I'm bare to my waist. The rest of me is beneath the covers. He's seen my breasts before. Touched them. Still, I feel bare and vulnerable.

And beautiful. The way he looks at me, his gaze hooded and dark, tells me he wants me. Me!

"I'll get you back on the sex wagon, but know this. I'm not doing it as a one-time thing. I'm all in, baby. We do this, you're mine."

I raise my head to meet his dark gaze.

"What?" I ask.

"I'm not doing this with you so you have confidence to go back to ladies' night and pick up some rando. I don't share."

"I wouldn't—"

"You *won't*." He grabs the sheet and yanks, pulling the whole thing off the bed and into a heap on the floor.

I gasp and he grabs an ankle, easily slides me across the bed so I'm lying sideways on the mattress facing him. He sets my foot on the edge of the bed, my knee bent toward the ceiling.

I'm quiet as he moves me to his liking, putting my other leg in the same position.

Now I'm not just naked but exposed. He can see *everything*.

"You won't because when I'm done with you, you'll be sore and thinking about my dick all week. How I crammed you full, made you come. Made you forget your own name. But you won't forget mine. My name will be branded into your memory."

I love what he's saying. I had no idea I like dirty talk, but wow. He's only touched my ankle so far and I'm dripping for him. I feel it on my thighs and as it trickles down between my legs.

"Just do it," I tell him, not even trying to be coy.

He slowly shakes his head and drops to his knees.

Oh my God.

He's right between my spread legs. His warm breath fans my heated flesh.

"This is the prettiest pussy I've ever seen."

I lift my head and look down my bare body to meet his eyes.

I don't think too much about all the other pussies he's seen.

"You don't like something, you tell me. Right away. Yeah?"

I nod.

"You do like something, I want to know that, too. Yell. Gasp. Hell, tug my hair."

I smile. "Less talk, more action, Austin."

He grins. "Yes, ma'am."

Then his mouth is on me.

"Holy shit!" I say aloud, because oh. My. God.

He licks and sucks and flicks with his tongue and then gets his fingers involved and there is nothing, *nothing,* about what he's doing that I don't like. In fact, I like it so much that I'm already close to coming.

I do as he said and shout how much I like what he's doing, how he's doing it and giving him directions of *harder* and *more* and *right there*. I even tug on his hair as he brings me to a screaming orgasm.

He pauses as I come down from my high. I glance down at him.

He sees the scars on my inner thighs.

And I'm still so fucking relaxed from the climax I don't even care.

A few seconds later, he licks and nibbles his way up my body as I catch my breath. He laves one nipple and then the other, before leaning over me and kissing the hell out of me.

I can taste my arousal and it's so hot.

"More?" he asks, kissing the spot behind my ear.

"More." I roll my hips.

"Be right back." The bed bounces as he pushes off and heads—bare assed—into the ensuite bathroom. He quickly returns with a condom and rolls it on.

I'm lying just where he left me, although I dropped one foot to the floor. He looms over me, studies me for a moment before scooping me up and shifting us on the bed so he's sitting up, back against the headboard. I'm in his lap, my legs straddling his waist. We're eye to eye and our gazes meet and hold.

"Climb on, baby. Take my dick for a ride."

He's hard and thick between us and I take him in hand. He hisses and his dick pulses against my palm. He wants me to be on top, to be free to move and do what feels good. I'm not held down. Not under him.

For some reason, this endears me to him even more. While this position, the idea of riding him like a cowgirl, is hot, he chose it for a reason.

Me.

I push up onto my knees so I'm hovering over him. Our gazes are still locked as I shift a little, lowering myself down so the broad head is at my entrance.

"Ready?" I ask.

"I've been waiting my whole life for this."

I don't think he's serious, so I don't respond. Only slowly lower onto him. He enters me, fills me. Stretches me. I grip his shoulders for balance as I raise and lower myself, taking him an inch at a time until I'm completely full.

He sets his feet on the bed and bends his knees so I sit in the cradle of his body.

He gently pushes between my breasts so I lean back against his thighs.

"Oh!" I cry, the rest of him sinking into me with this adjusted angle.

"Fuck, baby. Stop that or this will be over before we start."

I'm clenching down around him. He's thick and it's just shy of painful the way he fills me.

"I can't help it," I whisper, and then I start to move.

He settles his hands on my hips, helping me lift and lower.

It feels so good. Amazing because he got me all primed with that first orgasm. I'm sensitive and swollen and three-quarters toward coming again. It's nothing like...

"Hey." He cups my breasts.

I didn't realize my eyes fell closed but I meet his dark gaze.

"Look at me. Keep those green eyes open. It's you and me. Just us."

I nod and chase my orgasm as our gazes hold. I circle my hips as I lower, my clit rubbing against him. I move faster, and then faster still.

Sweat slicks our skin.

"I'm close," I tell him, but somehow it's just out of reach.

He licks his thumb and settles it between us so it hits my clit every time I shift.

"Oh," I moan. Yes, that little bit of extra pressure is what I was missing.

I fuck myself down onto him, hard and steady, and then I'm there.

I scream and hope Miles was right and that he and Chance can't hear me. Because there's no way I can keep these sounds in. It's amazing, the feel of Austin.

Him inside me.

Us.

He thrusts up to meet me, hard. His breathing is ragged and his motions become wild, no rhythm. He's chasing his own satisfaction and in one, two deep thrusts, he holds himself deep. And he comes.

"Oh my God," I breathe, falling onto his chest.

He wraps his arms around me, holding me close. He's still deep inside me and I smile.

This. Right here.

Everything.

I'm not sure how long we lie there together, entwined. I only know that I feel safe and happy.

Austin hasn't moved either.

And I feel complete.

I feel right.

And I never want to move.

17

USTIN

"Austin!"

Hands grip my shoulders. Carly's hands.

I jerk upward to banging on my bedroom door.

For a moment, I'm back home in Seattle, and the alarm is going off for the early morning cargo run.

But this isn't Seattle.

And I have a gorgeous woman in my bed. Whose every soft inch I can feel against me. Who came like a dream when I was inside her. Who has so many issues I don't know where to start, although perhaps it's a conversation about the scars on her thighs and back. I couldn't ask her yesterday, not in the middle of something she and I both wanted. So I figure I'd ask her later, in the afterglow. They sure as shit aren't going anywhere.

Except the afterglow included the best sleep I've had in forty Sundays, and apparently it was pretty good for her too, since it's morning and she's still here.

But she's no longer asleep. She's holding my shoulders with the grip of death.

"Knock it off!" I yell to whoever's pounding.

"Open up." It's Miles. His deep voice carries through the door. "I need to talk to you."

"I'm a little busy," I say.

What the hell time is it, anyway? I glance at the window. It's light out, but the sun rises before six.

Carly unclenches her hands from my flesh and crawls out of the other side of the bed, pulling a sheet around her, and races into the bathroom, closing the door.

O...kay.

At least I don't have to explain what she's doing here, although Miles isn't stupid. I scramble into my jeans but don't bother with the button and open the door. "What the fuck do you want?"

Miles, also wearing nothing but a pair of jeans, barges into my room, looking around. I had no idea he had a tattoo on his chest. "Thank God. Rick Vance is here and he's about ready to blow a freaking gasket. He's looking for— Oh, Fuck. She's still here." Miles's gaze falls on Carly's clothes neatly stacked on the chair by the window.

"Yeah. She's in the bathroom," I say quietly. "And none of this is any of her father's business."

He runs a hand down his face, his hand rasping over his whiskers. "Agreed. She's over eighteen, but the fact remains that he's here, and he's convinced that she is, too. I was hoping he was wrong because dealing with a pissed off Daddy…"

I shake my head, feeling fiercely protective of my woman, regardless of who's out there. "I'm not going to apologize."

His eyes widen. "Who asked you to?"

I frown. "Chance will. He'll want me to kiss Vance's ass, but that's never been my style."

"Say what you want about Chance, but he's no ass kisser either."

I run a hand through my hair. "Okay, you're right. But he's a do-gooder."

"Do-gooder?" Miles laughs. "You really just used that term?"

I ignore him and walk to the chair, pick up Carly's clothes, and take them to the bathroom. I knock softly.

She opens the door a crack and I hand her the clothes. "How much have you heard?" I ask.

"Just bits and pieces, but I got the gist. My father is here, isn't he?"

"Apparently."

She sighs and pulls the clothes close to her body, which is a fucking pity because if I had my way, she wouldn't get dressed again for a while. "I'll be out in a minute."

"You don't have to do this," I tell her. I want to stroke her hair. Kiss her swollen lips. Hell, get her beneath me in bed again. "You don't owe him any explanation."

She looks away and nods. "I do, though. He and I were supposed to talk this morning at breakfast, and I... Well, obviously I wasn't there. I'm an adult, but I do live with them. I owe them the courtesy of at least a text or something to let them know where I am. After... well, after what I went through, they deserve that much."

I can't help but agree. Even if it means she dresses and leaves.

"I may have sneaked in here with a plan, but I didn't mean to stay all night, Austin."

"I didn't mean for it to happen either," I admit, "but it did, and I fucking loved the surprise." I give in and caress her messy hair—hair that's mussed because she was in my bed. "I'm not sorry."

A small smile turns up the corner of her mouth. "I'm

not either. But I do owe my dad an explanation as to why I wasn't at breakfast. God, how did I let this happen?"

"Carly..."

"I'll just be a minute." She closes the door between us.

I sigh and turn. Miles still stands just inside my bedroom.

"What do you want me to tell Chance and Mayor Vance?" he asks.

I shake my head, running my fingers through my hair again. "Tell them that this isn't eighth grade and my sex life isn't any of their business."

"You got it." Miles grips the doorknob.

"No, wait." I hold up a hand and sigh.

He turns.

Mayor Vance is Carly's father. He means something to her, and she means something to me.

Hell, she means a *lot* to me.

If we'd known each other for more than a damned week, I'd say I'm falling for her. But how can I be? Love at first sight doesn't exist.

Except I feel like a wolf who needs to protect his mate.

But protect her from whom?

The only other person who wants her safety as much as I do. Her father.

"I'm aging here," Miles says. "Vance isn't going to wait

forever in the other room. Soon enough, he'll start searching."

"I need to put on something more than jeans. I'll be out in a minute."

"With Carly?"

"That's up to her."

He turns toward the door. "Good enough. I'll tell them you're coming. The mayor and Chance are in the living room."

"Wait, wait, wait... You're not going to be there?"

"This doesn't concern me, bro."

"It doesn't concern either of them either."

Miles lets out a laugh. "Good point."

"Look," I say. "You and I don't know each other at all, but if there's something good to come out of this, it's that I have a brother who I think I might like."

He rolls his eyes. "You're a fucking sweet talker. I'm blushing."

"For fuck's sake. That came out all wrong. I need you, man. I need you on my side out there. I'd do the same for you. I swear it."

He cocks his head and studies me. "Yeah, I think you would. Get some damned clothes on and meet me in the living room. You're right. I'm not missing this showdown for anything."

"Ha. Funny." I push him out of the room and hastily

dress in a clean shirt. I slide my leather slippers onto my feet. Then I kick them off and put on socks and my jogging shoes. Slippers mean I just got up. They mean I was in bed. Jogging shoes mean—

Oh, fuck. Like it matters.

Carly emerges from the bathroom, her silky hair pulled back in a high ponytail. Yeah, one look at her and it won't matter. She looks freshly fucked no matter how much effort she puts in.

"I borrowed your comb. I hope you don't mind."

I frown. "Why would I mind?"

"My mom hates when I borrow hers. She says I get my long hair stuck in it."

"Well, I don't care." I draw in a deep breath. "You don't have to go out there."

"Yeah," she says. "I do."

"You sure, baby? Because I can take this for you. I'm happy to."

"You don't know my dad. If I don't produce myself he'll search this whole house."

"Which is thirty shades of illegal," I say. "Based on the interaction with your dad yesterday, I'd say he's a man with respect for the law."

"He is. But where I'm concerned, the line between law and chaos gets a little blurry."

I cup her cheek. "God, you feel like silk." I sigh. "I get

it. He doesn't want to lose you again."

"No, he doesn't. I understand that. But I need to stand on my own two feet, and he has to understand *that*." She places her hand over mine and then slides it off her cheek. "However this ends up, I don't regret last night, Austin. I'll never regret last night."

"Wait... What do you mean, *however* this ends up? I told you I'm all in, Carly. I meant it."

"I know you did." She gives a weak smile. "But you deserve better than a woman who's broken." She brushes past me and out the door.

What the fuck?

I grab her arm and yank her back into my bedroom. "Don't you dare," I say. "Don't you dare tell me this is over. Not after you commandeered my bed last night. Not after—"

The whites of her eyes glisten, but no tears fall. "I'm still healing."

"I know that, Carly. Damn!" I rub at my jawline, my heart doing backflips. "None of that matters to me. Only you. *You* matter. And maybe we haven't known each other that long, but I already know you're not the kind of woman who uses a guy for sex."

"I didn't used to be."

"You still aren't," I practically snap. "You aren't."

Maybe if I say it enough, she'll begin to believe it.

Because *I* believe it. Carly is a beautiful woman, inside and out. A good soul. She wouldn't have gone to bed with me just to practice.

And God help me if she did.

Because damn... Fucking God damn...

She whisks past me again, and this time I let her go.

I sure as hell am following her, though. We're in this together, whether she likes it or not. One night wasn't enough. Hell, I'm not sure if one lifetime will be.

18

ARLY

MY HEART IS RACING, but not out of fear.

I *know* fear. I lived fear for three years.

This isn't that. This is just me trying to figure out how to best handle this situation without harming Austin or his brothers.

Last night was amazing. I'm a little sore from it because Austin is big. He was also rough, which was what I wanted. I never wanted rose petals and soft music. No, he got me so mindless I pretty much forgot my own name. Just as he said I would.

I was everything a woman was supposed to be when

with a man. Aroused, uninhibited, passionate. Needy. Achy. Desperate.

I want more from him, but it's not simple. My father came here looking for me. Here!

Where else did he go? How much time has he spent trying to find me?

I walk calmly—as calmly as I can—through the hallway, past the kitchen, and into the large front room. Austin doesn't leave my side because I feel his presence, and his hand at the small of my back.

As soon as we enter—

"Carly!" Dad races toward me and grabs me into a hug. "Thank God."

I feel the worry dissipating from him, the way he holds me tight. The way he exhales.

In a moment, though, the anger will emerge. The only question is whether it will be directed at me or at Austin.

Except it's not a question at all.

I hold my breath and wait.

Dad releases me, and his dark eyes burn into Austin, who's standing next to me. "What the hell is my daughter doing with you? Carly, did you spend the night here?"

"With all due respect, sir," Austin says, "that isn't your business."

Miles shows up then, fully dressed and his concerned gaze on Austin. He says nothing.

Chance rubs at his forehead as if someone just split it open with an ax. He wasn't happy the last time Austin had his hands on me and he's clearly not happy now. "Jesus Christ, Austin."

Chance is the least of my worries because my dad's about to freak.

Here it comes.

Before I see it, I feel it. My father's rage.

"The hell it's not!" Dad advances on Austin, poking a finger into his chest.

But Austin stands his ground and he grabs my hand. My dad's practically breathing down his neck and he's taken my hand to reassure me.

I swallow. "I'm a grown woman, Daddy." I clear my throat and speak louder. "I'm sorry about breakfast. I didn't mean to miss it, but—"

"Did you forget *why* we were going to have breakfast together?" Dad demands. "To talk about the Bridgers and why I think you should stay away from them."

Austin drops my hand. "Carly?"

I gulp audibly. "We were to talk about *Jonathan* Bridger and why he took our land."

"They're all Bridgers," Dad counters, glaring at Austin.

Here I am again, stuck between a rock and a hard place. Daddy and Austin.

Daddy, who's protected me—or tried to—his whole life.

And Austin, who I've known for less than a week, but who has shown me I'm still desirable, still able to feel. The ache between my thighs is a reminder of that.

My choice should be a no-brainer.

But it's not.

Not even slightly. Because Austin said that once he took me, I was his. I was already naked when he told me that. He didn't have to proclaim it because having sex was a sure thing.

Therefore, he meant it, even though I'm clearly fucked up and have a fucked-up family.

Even so, I love my father, but I also...

No. It's not possible that I love Austin. It's too soon. Sex isn't love.

But Austin was so caring, so willing to do whatever I needed. He's not standing down from my dad, willing to face his anger head on. He's not interested in a one nighter because what man would face my dad otherwise?

And now? I'm not interested in only one night either.

I can't—I *won't*—give Austin up. Not because he knows how to do things with his tongue that are probably illegal in some states. Or that he makes me feel alive. Feminine. Pretty.

He makes me feel whole for the first time in...years.

Still, I will hear my father out about the Bridgers. I owe and respect him that much.

I turn to Austin. "I need to know why he's so dead set against your family, me working here. All of it."

"You working here is now the least of my concerns," Dad says gruffly. "I wanted to keep you out of this mess, but I can see they got to you too. Let's go. I'm taking you home."

The little girl in me—the one who cried on that island for her daddy to come rescue her—wants desperately to obey.

But the woman—the empowered twenty-seven-year-old woman—knows I cannot.

I must stand my ground. If I don't now, I never will.

I shake my head. "I love you, Daddy, and I do want to hear what you have to say, but I'm not coming with you."

A vein throbs in his temple. I don't remember seeing him this angry before, not even when I told him I was working at this ranch.

"What the hell did you to do her, Bridger?" Dad advances on Austin once more.

I slide my body between them, stopping his attack. I grip my dad's upper arm. "No. He didn't do anything, and I don't want you talking to him like that."

"It's okay, Carly," Austin murmurs in my ear.

"No, it's not okay, it's—"

"She's safe here," Miles says. "No one will ever hurt her with us near."

"Damn straight," Austin whispers.

Chance nods.

"Three against one?" Dad practically growls.

I want to roll my eyes but know that won't help.

Austin steps forward, effectively sandwiching me between them so I have no choice but to step aside if I don't want to be crushed.

"There is no fight here, Mr. Vance."

"I ought to kick you into next week," Dad snarls.

Austin huffs. "I'd like to see you try. You sure wouldn't get very far. And for what, exactly? Loving on your daughter?"

I melt at the question, but only for a second.

Dad ruins it by saying, "You touched her?"

"Oh, for God's sake!" I curl my hands into fists. "Stop it, both of you! This isn't an elementary school playground and my sex life is *not* up for discussion."

"Sex?" Dad looks close to having a stroke.

"Carly..." Austin's voice cuts over my dad's harsh tone.

"No. Enough. Daddy, I spent the night here. With Austin. That's my business. And his. No one else's." I look to Chance as well, making sure he understands he needs to lay off. "We fell asleep and I missed having breakfast with you, which wasn't my intention."

"You planned to what... Fuck and flee?" Dad says on a snarl.

I gasp at his crude words.

"Don't disrespect your daughter like that," Austin commands.

I'm taken aback by what my dad said, but I won't stand down. Not now. Still, I have to blink back tears. "Not that I owe you an explanation, but I'm very sorry I missed our breakfast." I turn to Austin. "And Austin? Don't you ever talk to my father like that again."

Austin opens his mouth—

"No," I say. "Don't say he threatened you first. I heard it, and I'm mad as hell at him for it. Both of you should know better."

"Baby, I won't let anyone talk about you like that, even your father," Austin says. "However, we're on the same side, caring about you. Mr. Vance, I apologize."

"It's Mayor Vance," Dad says, "and you should be apologizing to Carly."

"He has no reason to apologize to me." I whip my hand to my hips. "He's done nothing wrong. In fact, he's done everything right."

That doesn't make my dad any happier.

I push on. "You should apologize to *him*."

Dad scoffs. "Not in this lifetime."

"Then we're done here. Unless you want to tell me

how you ended up here in the first place. Did you search every house in town or come straight here?"

"I don't trust them," Dad says.

I tip up my chin. "I do."

"You don't know everything."

"Go, Dad. Go home. You can tell me all about why you hate the Bridgers so much, but standing here, in their house? It's not okay."

Austin's hand settles on my hip again and he gives it a squeeze. I'm reassured, but it doesn't feel good to tell my dad off.

His lips thin into a straight line. He glares at Austin, and then at Chance and Miles in turn. He sets his hat back on his head, turns, and storms out. The front door slams in his wake.

No one moves. My father sucked all the oxygen from the room with his departure.

Austin's pocket starts playing "Superwoman" by Alicia Keys. He pulls out his phone and immediately answers it.

"Mom. Is everything ok?"

I look up at him as he listens. He didn't look the least bit worried facing off with my dad, but he does now.

"What? Are you fucking kidding me?"

 USTIN

AFTER WHAT JUST WENT DOWN, I hate leaving Carly with her dad all pissed. Even to talk to my mom. So I don't. I tag her hand when she thinks to step away from me and wrap my arm around her. She looks up at me but stays quiet.

The guys already know about my mom. The last time she and I talked—we texted a few times since—I was in Chance's truck headed into town.

Carly knows about Mom's illness. This call though, isn't about that because...

Fuck.

"Are you sure?" I ask.

"Sure that Greg secretly works for Sea-Air and has been taking on our flights to steal our transport clients? Yes. I'm sure."

Greg was hired to be my fill-in while I'm in Montana, to take all the routes I usually fly. That includes passengers who reserved travel through our website, and also cargo—like the day Shankle showed up and I was shuffling oysters to a client.

"How many?"

"So far? Five."

"Five?" I tip my head back and stare at the ceiling.

Five transport routes gone.

"Who's the owner of Sea-Air again?" I ask.

"Frank Parcell," she replies.

"Right. The asshole hears about me going to Montana and... what? Decides to finish us?"

I hear her frustrated sigh through the miles.

"He knows I'm sick. That's not news at this point. I don't know how he learned about your father's will though."

I think on it. "It's got to be Ed."

"From the dock?" Surprise laces Mom's words.

I nod even though she can't see me. "He was there when Shankle showed up. I can't remember how much Shankle shared before we took off, but I do know he overheard that Jonathan Bridger died."

"So he put two and two together."

"I did leave within the month," I remind her. "I doubt Ed did anything on purpose. He probably just mentioned my situation to Frank in passing. I mean, we've known him forever."

Mom is quiet for a minute. "What are we going to do?"

"You're not going to do anything. Not even worry," I say.

She laughs.

Carly, Chance, and Miles are staring at me, concerned.

"Is your mom okay?" Carly whispers.

I put my hand over the phone. "She's fine. The fucker we hired to fill in was a mole and stole our routes."

"You're not alone," Mom says, apparently realizing I'm updating the others. "I'm sorry, sweetheart."

I take my hand away. "It's fine. It's Chance, Miles, and Carly."

"Who's Carly?"

Yes, I hear the curiosity in her voice. The one that always comes out when a woman is involved, because that's the key to her desire for grandchildren.

"You want to ask me that now?" I pose.

I need to get Mom back on track. She wants to know about the woman in my life when a sneaky bastard is taking advantage of her and stealing our business.

Mom sighs again. "It's done. He's fired. Obviously."

"Obviously."

"But without a pilot, no flights are going up now. I had to cancel the passengers for today, which means they got their money back *and* went to another company."

"Sea-Air probably," I grumble. "I can send you money to pay bills, but without routes—without a *pilot*—we're doomed. I'd say hire another one but who knows who we can trust at this point."

Carly looks up at me and gives me a reassuring smile. It doesn't solve anything, but it sure as fuck feels good.

I notice Chance on his cell now, pacing the length of the room.

"I'll come back," I say to Mom. "I'll fly them."

"What? No. You can't. The will says—"

"Jonathan Bridger can't keep controlling our lives, Mom."

"It's a *billion* dollars," she counters. "Even if the company goes under—"

"It won't."

"But with that money, does it matter?"

I stiffen and Carly steps back.

"Mom, do you want Sea-Air to win? Do you want the company you started to fail now because Jonathan Bridger, the guy who abandoned you when you were pregnant, dictates me being here even when he's dead?"

"When you put it that way," she says with a forced laugh.

"There's got to be a way."

"There is," Chance interrupts. He's done with his phone call and comes over.

I look to him, but I speak into the cell. "Hang on a sec, Mom."

"Shankle says you can't go back to Seattle," he replies. "It'll break the will."

I'm not sure how this is remotely helpful and I'm about to say that, but he continues.

"But *we* can. Remember he said there were stipulations about us leaving? You, me, and Miles. Together." He points between the three of us. "I know it's ridiculous, but apparently our esteemed father said we can leave in the case of an emergency, though he didn't define what an emergency was. Shankle says as far as he's concerned this qualifies, but we have to go together, and only for a week at a time."

Miles widens his eyes, and he smiles. "Fuck, yeah."

I frown at both of them. "Can either of you fly a plane?"

Chance looks at me as if I asked him if he works for a circus. "Hell, no."

Miles shakes his head.

"But *you* can," Chance adds.

Miles steps closer. "Yeah. If what we're hearing is all of it, we can help you find a new pilot while you're taking those trips. One who isn't a thieving dick."

Chance's smile spreads. "I'm happy to track down this Greg asshole and let him know there's more than one Bridger now."

I think Chance has a need to beat the shit out of someone. I'm glad it's moved on from me to someone more... deserving.

"You two want to move to Seattle? I thought we're supposed to run the ranch together. That we have to stay in Montana."

"I didn't say move," Chance says. "Per Shankle, all we get is a week. Then we have to be back here to continue to meet the rules of the will."

Carly nods. Doing this means a week away from her, but I don't have much choice.

"You hear all that, Mom?"

"I did. It's a start."

"Then I guess I'll see you soon. I'll be in touch. You just take care of yourself, okay?" I end the call.

Carly stands next to me, her hand still in mine. "So you're leaving..."

I pull her away from Chance and Miles so we have a bit of privacy. "Only for a week, sweetheart."

"You might forget me in a week." She looks down at my chest.

I tip her chin up. "That is not going to happen."

She sighs. "I won't forget you, for sure. I do have to go talk to my father."

"So you can get the lowdown on the evil Bridgers." I grin.

"Whatever he says, I know it has nothing to do with you, but..."

"But...you need to hear him out."

"I do. I need to learn what he knows. I'd much rather go to Seattle with you."

"God, I wish..." I kiss the top of her head and then I hand her my phone. "Program your number in. I don't want to be out of touch with you for a second. You need me, I'm a call away."

She adds her number and hands the phone back. I tap on her name and her phone rings in her pocket. "Now you have my number, too. Call me anytime, baby. I mean it."

"I will. When are you leaving?"

"I have no idea. I have to talk to Chance and Miles. Tonight if possible, I suppose. If we can get a flight."

Chance shakes her head, chuckling. "Did you forget already?"

I wrinkle my forehead. "Forget what?"

"We can leave anytime we want. We Bridgers have our own private jet."

My jaw drops. Damn. He said something about a plane that first day when we all met, made some snide comment about training wheels.

Carly touches my cheek. "You, Austin, have your own plane."

"Can we even use it?"

If Shankle says the three of us only get a small stipend each month, maybe there are rules for other things as well.

"The ranch trust has all the money it needs to run. The will's stipulations are only to fuck with us," Chance adds.

"What about the money being tied up because of dear old Dad's EPA violations?"

"As far as I know, nothing has been frozen yet," Chance replies. "Shankle didn't say anything about it just now."

Fuck. Another problem. This is all a giant pain in the ass. Except for one thing.

Carly.

I want to stay here. Here, with her.

How the hell did I get to this point?

"Come with us," I say to her.

She opens her eyes wide.

"I'm serious," I continue. "I don't want to leave you for a week. Come along. Chance and Miles won't mind."

"I would if I could, but you know I have to see my dad. And I have a job with a pain-in-the-ass boss." She gives me a light punch in the arm.

I laugh. "He'll understand."

She shakes her head. "No. I have a job. And my dad's going to be even more upset if I go. I need to get that handled."

I sigh. "I know. But I had to try." I glance over at my brothers.

Chance is on the phone again, and I motion to Miles. He walks toward Carly and me.

"What's the plan?" I ask.

"Chance is setting us up to leave tonight. On our plane." Miles adds.

"What about the Feds? What about that dam Mayor Vance was bitching about? What about the damned ranch?"

"Hell if I know," Miles says, "but if Shankle and Chance say it's okay, I guess it is."

"Sure enough. I'm going to take Carly home. I'll be back as soon as I can."

 ARLY

To my complete surprise, Austin actually drives me home.

Not home, actually, but into town, to the City Hall building.

I turn to him when he stops the car out front. I could've asked him sooner, but I zoned out the window and thought about what we did. How my body is still humming from it.

I am sore, but in a delicious way. I'm going to feel what we did all day. Maybe longer.

"What's this?" I ask.

"Your dad's office, isn't it? I assumed you wanted to talk to him."

"I do, but he could be in a meeting for all I know. He keeps pretty busy."

I also didn't want to have another public fight with him. If he's going to be hot-headed, the mayor's office isn't the best spot. I'm also not quite ready to face him. I want him to cool off some, to think and hopefully see some reason.

"In this one-horse town?"

"Well, yeah. He's in charge of the county, too."

"All right. Just tell me where you want to go. I should know the way to your family's property anyway."

I chew on my lip and look at Austin. Less than a few hours ago, I was sleeping next to him—before Miles pounded on the door.

The thing is, I don't want to face my dad, but I don't want to go home either. All that will happen is that my mom will stare at me anxiously and I'll feel awful for spending the night with Austin. She won't slut-shame me or anything, but I'm sure she'll be thinking about the fact that I was with a man, all night.

What I want to do is return to the ranch and work. Lexie needs me this week, especially since the other vet is off. Plus when I'm with the animals, I forget about everything. They don't talk back. Or wonder what's wrong with me. Or look at me with worry or pity.

It wasn't fair of my father to try to get me to quit—rather, to quit on my behalf—and I'm furious about it. I finally convinced Lexie that I could do more than groom horses and feed puppies and now this.

I want to work, damn it.

And I want to work on Bridger Ranch.

"Don't kick my butt," I say, "but let's go back to your place."

He grins. "Now you're talking, and baby, I love your butt."

I punch him good-naturedly in his upper arm. "I mean to work. My *job*. Besides, I left my car there last night and I'll need it."

He shakes his head and laughs. "I didn't even think of how you got to my bed. I admit, seeing you there, naked, scrambled my brain."

"My car's by the stable. I didn't think leaving it in front of your house was much of a surprise."

"It was a surprise. The best one." He winks.

I blush, agreeing. "My father may have tried to have me quit, but *I* didn't. I love that job, and I think I'll be really good at it, if I can stay on long enough to prove myself."

"Why do you want to work on the ranch?" he asks.

"I love animals. I was a vet student, before..."

He reaches out and cups my cheek. "Oh. I'm sorry."

"Please. Don't be. I have to learn that it's okay to say the words. I was in my first year of vet school. I hope I can go back someday, but that may require moving to a different state."

Funny. Just days ago I was considering leaving Bayfield. Now? You'd have to drag me kicking and screaming away from Austin. Is it smart or plain stupid to put my plans on a guy?

"Where did you go before?" he asks.

"Colorado State University. I was here at home during spring break, and that's when..." I clear my throat. "That's when I was abducted from the bathroom in Millie's Diner."

"Oh, baby..."

I draw in a breath. "It's okay. It was two years ago now since I was rescued. I've been through a year of intensive therapy and I still see a doctor once or twice a month. I'm good, Austin. But I need to work. It helps."

He kicks the sedan back into gear. "Then back to work you'll go."

I cover one of his hands with my own. "Yes. That's what I want, but...you know what I want even more?"

He lifts his eyebrows. "What?"

"You."

"Oh baby," he groans, "those are fighting words."

"Definitely not right here in front of City Hall. But if you're leaving tonight," I say, biting my lip, "I want to be with you before you go."

"What about your job?" He waggles his eyebrows.

"Lexie will understand."

Yeah, she sure will. I owe it to women everywhere to be with a guy as amazing—and skilled—as Austin Bridger. I'll be a little late. And a little blissed out.

———

WE SNEAK back into the house without Miles or Chance seeing us, and as soon as we are back in Austin's room, the door closed and locked behind us, he pushes me against the wall, his hands holding my arms above my head.

"Okay?" he asks.

"Don't stop," I shift in his hold.

He crushes his mouth to mine. The kiss is firm, open-mouthed, and drugging, and I melt into it, embracing Austin's strength. Needing it. Craving it.

Our lips slide together, our tongues tangle, and our teeth clash, and my God...

It's so raw in its intensity, and I squirm, attempting to ease the ache between my legs. I'm already so worked up and we've only kissed.

I'm still sore from last night. A good burning sore, and I want more. I want him to burn through me like fire. Especially if he's leaving.

I yearn to grab his bulge, cup him, but he's holding my arms above my head. I try to wrangle free but he groans into my mouth and then breaks the kiss.

"Bad girl," he says huskily.

God, that lights me up. I've always been a good girl, doing what I'm supposed to. Those two words are a kink I didn't even know I'd like.

"Please," I whimper. "I want to touch you, Austin."

"Oh, you will, baby. We will touch every inch of each other, but damn. I have to have you. Like this. Up against the wall. This one's going to be fast."

He finally lets my arms go, but when I reach to cup him, he moves away. "So greedy."

He strips in record time. His huge cock bobs against his belly, long and thick. I didn't see much of him the night before, but now, in daylight, he's impressive.

Oh God. My pussy is throbbing. Aching and clenching in need.

"Take off your shoes, Carly. Then your jeans. Then your panties. Fuck, take it all off. I want you naked. I want those gorgeous tits free."

I tremble as I obey him without question while he rolls on a condom he pulled from the back pocket of his jeans. I watch, but in this moment I focus on getting bare. I want only to obey him. Only to—

He sucks in a breath. "God, you're fucking beautiful."

He stalks toward me, and in a flash I'm back against the wall. He cups my ass and lifts me. Automatically, I wrap my legs around his waist. In one motion, he pushes down and thrusts his hips up, driving his dick into me.

I cry out, the feeling so intense. So full.

I close my eyes and tilt my head back. He clamps his lips onto my neck as he thrusts, thrusts, thrusts.

"Fuck, Carly. You feel so good." His breath fans my heated skin.

Each thrust nudges his chest against my hard nipples and his lower body scrapes against my clit.

It's wild. Feral even. His ragged breathing shows he's just as lost in this as I am.

He's bigger than the vibrator. More. He wraps around me, the hard wall at my back cool in comparison to his heat.

I climb higher and higher, until—

"Austin!" I burst into a climax so intense it radiates outward, to my fingers and toes, and then back to my core as my walls clench.

"Fuck, that's so tight. You're killing me."

"It's so good," I moan. Because it is.

"That's it, my Carly. Come. Come for me."

Austin continues to thrust as I let the last threads of my climax tingle through me. With each plunge, he buries himself more deeply inside me, and I feel everything last millimeter of him as I pulse around him.

"Fuck," he grits out. "Fuck!"

He thrusts hard, and I'm so in sync with him that I feel him swell inside me before he holds himself deep and lets go. A deep, guttural growl escapes his chest as he slaps a hand against the wall beside my head.

I'm breathing hard, little aftershocks of pleasure pulsing through me. I want to stay like this forever. Held up and protected by him. Feeling him inside me. The two of us connected as one.

He stays there for a moment, embedded deep, his forehead wet from perspiration, and he leans against me, his eyes closed. Lost.

Another moment, and he pulls away slightly, helping my feet to the ground. His rough palms rake over my body. My shoulders, my breasts, waist. Hips, thighs.

I still when he comes in contact with the raised marks.

"Carly..." he says softly.

"Austin," I reply.

"We need to talk about those scars." His fingers stroke over one of them.

Just like that, I'm jerked out of my orgasmic bliss. He

heads to the bathroom to deal with the condom, which doesn't take long enough.

I shake my head when he returns. "Please. Not now. I thought—"

He kisses my lips—just a light brushing—and then takes my hand and leads me to the bed. He sits down and pats the area beside him.

"I'm okay," I say, as if he'll hopefully accept that as the answer and move on to round two.

"I know you are. And you're beautiful to me."

Why do we have to do this?

We're naked. On a bed. Not having sex.

"Every part of you," he continues. "But if you need to talk about any of it—"

I shake my head. "I don't, not with you."

He takes my hand, entwines our fingers together. "I'm falling hard for you, Carly Vance, and I need to know."

He's so wonderful...and I'm such a mess.

But when Austin Bridger looks at me, I don't feel scarred. I don't feel like... less than whole. I don't feel damaged.

I feel like the most beautiful woman in the world.

"You can help just by being yourself," I tell him. "That's what no one seems to understand. What would help me the most is if everyone would just treat me like a normal person. I'm not just talking about you. I mean my parents, Lexie, Chance, everyone. Yes, I've been through hell, but I came out kicking, and I'm ready to just be normal again."

"Oh baby, I don't see you that way. I just don't want to hurt you."

"If I need anything, I'll tell you. I'm not too proud to ask for help. But what I need right now is for you not to treat me like that fragile little puppy of Duchess's who has to be bottle-fed. I'm scarred, yes, but I'm healing." I breathe in, let it out slowly. "I'm sorry I told you I was damaged. I'm not. You proved it to me. I can still feel, and it's a wonderful thing."

"Fuck, yeah. Baby, you make me feel too. More than I ever thought I could."

I push his hair off his forehead. "What do you mean?"

He chuckles. "I've never been serious when it comes to women, but you make me want to be. Hell, I already am with you."

Warmth surges through me. I can't possibly be in love with this man. Not yet.

So why do I feel like I've found my forever?

Of course it's someone my father doesn't want me anywhere near.

Which reminds me...

"God, I still I need to talk to my dad."

"I know."

"I need to see Lexie and tell her I'm all in with my job, no matter what my dad said. I'm late...again."

"Don't worry. She'll have you."

"Don't you dare put in a good word for me or make excuses for why I'm late. This is my responsibility, Austin."

He holds up his hands in mock surrender. "Okay, okay."

I rise and begin to dress.

"Such a shame to cover all those treats up," Austin says. "I didn't get to suck on those pretty little nipples."

"When you get back from Seattle, they'll be waiting. All of me will."

 ARLY

LEXIE'S in the vet's office when I arrive.

I'm leaning against the doorframe. "Hi."

She looks up from her paperwork, clearly flustered. "Oh, Carly. What are you doing here?"

I clench my fingers together, suddenly nervous. "Coming to work, if you'll have me."

"I got a phone call from your dad saying you no longer work here."

I cringe, imagining that conversation. "I know, and I have to apologize for that. My dad doesn't make my decisions for me. I'll understand if you want nothing to do with me after this mess, but I love this job and I want to work."

"I see."

"Have you hired anyone else?"

"I haven't had a minute to think about that." She smiles and sets a pen down on the messy desk.

The office is near the stables, and the ever-present scent of horses hangs in the air.

"The job is yours. We have a ton to do. Chance just told me they're going to break down the dam at Shipp's Creek, so we have to go out there and check for any wildlife that might be affected while they're gone to... I guess he didn't say where."

"Seattle," I say.

She widens her eyes. "Oh? Chance said all three Bridgers have to leave town for a week. Together."

I'm not sure how much I should say, so I don't reply.

"Anyway," Lexie says, "you up for checking out the area around the dam tomorrow?"

I nod. "Absolutely. I'll be here bright and early to feed the horses."

"Good," she says. "We'll head to the creek after that."

"Perfect. Do you need me for anything today?" *Please say yes.*

"You're a lifesaver," she says on a sigh. "Yes. I'm drowning in paperwork and I'm supposed to repair an umbilical hernia on one of the foals this afternoon. I hate to make you do busy work when I'm sure you'd rather be assisting me, but it has to get done."

"Not a problem." I smile. "I'm happy to help wherever I'm needed."

"You're an angel." Lexie pulls her phone out and checks it. "I'm glad you're back, Carly. Or, I'm glad you never left."

"Me, too."

The day goes quickly with never-ending chores, and I feel good when I'm done. Valued. Needed.

And not just by Austin, who I don't see again.

The drive to my parents' home seems longer than usual. Probably because I'm dreading the conversation I know is coming with my father. I sit in my car for another five minutes before I walk to the house.

I draw in a deep breath and enter, taking off my dirty boots in the mud room. Ernie pants happily and I ruffle his ears as he sniffs all the animal smells on my pants.

"You are just what I need right now, boy."

He gives me a few rough swipes of his tongue.

"Carly?" Mom calls from the kitchen. "Dinner's almost ready."

I walk in and inhale. "Tacos?"

"Your favorite." She smiles at me before turning back to the lettuce she's chopping into small shreds. "And your father's."

"Do you need help?" I walk to the sink to wash my hands.

"No, it's all under control. Dad is in his den. He wants to talk to you."

I feel nothing but dread. "I know. About last night..."

"Just go talk to Dad, okay?" Mom doesn't meet my gaze.

Yeah, she's just as I thought. I slept with a guy and it's hanging in the air between us.

"All right." I grab a diet soda out of the refrigerator and walk toward the den.

The door is closed, so I knock. "Daddy?"

"Come in, Carly."

I open the door. He's sitting behind the table he uses as a makeshift desk. His computer screen is dark, which is odd. When he's in the den, he's almost always on the computer. I expected him to have all kinds of documents pulled up to show me how horrible the Bridgers are. Evidence to prove his case against them.

"Sit down." He nods to a chair on the other side of the table.

I take the seat while I chew on my lower lip.

Here it comes.

"Where were you today?" he asks.

I clear my throat. "At work."

Silence for a moment, until—

"I see."

No blow up. No shouts of anger. I'm not sure if this empty stoicism is any better.

"I worked at Bridger Ranch. As usual. Dr. Davis is thrilled to have me. She needs me. She's swamped, with the other vet out."

I'm not sure why I'm explaining myself. I want to work at Bridger Ranch, so I'll work there.

"I see," Dad echoes. A pause, and then, "Jonathan Bridger was not a good man."

And it begins.

"I know that's what you think."

"That's what I *know*, Carly." He rises and comes around the table to sit next to me. "This will be difficult for you to hear."

"Whatever you say won't change my mind about working there. Or about Austin."

He shakes his head and takes a fortifying breath. "You can't say that. Not until I tell you the truth."

"I *can* say that, Daddy. I understand Mr. Bridger cheated you, but the brothers will make that right. I'm sure he cheated others, too. He probably broke the law. He probably did any number of things, but that was the father. Not the sons."

"Carly," Dad says, "have you ever wondered why you were abducted?"

I jerk in my chair. I spent a lot of the past two years asking myself that question, and I've finally come to terms that it doesn't matter because I can't change it. I can't erase the past. I can only move forward.

So I sure didn't expect it to come up in this conversation.

"I've been trying to figure it out since you disappeared, and a week ago, I finally got some relevant information."

I gulp. "Just say it, Daddy. Please."

"I've been working with an FBI agent since you went missing. Not much has come up since you returned, but we still talk. Last week, he called with some information that finally came across his desk."

"And...?" I whisper the word, unable to get it to come out any louder.

"He found the document naming all the individuals who visited Derek Wolfe's island. It was classified, but he got his hands on it two years after the fact. Most of them were fake names, including one the agent thought I'd be interested in." Dad pauses, threads his fingers through his graying hair. "It was an alias used by Jonathan Bridger."

A rock lands in my gut, and nausea begins the slow ascent up my throat.

"You don't mean..."

He nods once. "Jonathan Bridger had a connection to the place, Carly. He's most likely the reason you were taken."

 USTIN

I SLEPT the whole flight to Seattle. For once, I was a passenger instead of a pilot. I admit, the Bridger jet is fancy and very convenient. The seats are plush and ridiculously comfortable. Maybe I've just worked too hard lately trying to be a cowboy. Our latest fun was getting wet and filthy breaking up that dam that Vance is having a coronary about. It was a great time after screwing his daughter this morning.

While we were tossing logs and hefting river rock, Chance explained about water rights and that ours date back to the 1800s. The Bridgers' rights are the oldest in the area, meaning we have first dibs on water access, but we also aren't allowed to block off water flow completely for downstream properties.

The Bridgers obviously aren't beavers and we have no control over nature and how the animals decided to block the flow. I know that well enough with weather and flying in the Pacific Northwest. But I appreciate how Chance wants to stay on Vance's good side, and even more to be a good neighbor.

So we spent a few hours decimating a dam in a creek. Only then did we head to the local airport and fly to Seattle.

I never expected to return home with my brothers in tow, like two pieces of oversized luggage. Yet here we are, at my mother's house and being fed mass quantities of homemade fried chicken. She knows it's my favorite, so she didn't skimp.

"Eat up, boys. I don't know where you'll put it, but I assume you'll be like your half brother and have hollow legs."

We're seated at her kitchen table, which is tight with the four of us.

"It's really great, Ms. Lovering," Miles says, waving a perfectly fried wing in the air. "Is there a hot sauce in the batter?"

She smiles and points her fork at him. "You bet there is."

I grab the bowl of potato salad and scoop some onto my plate. I hold the bowl in my mom's direction, silently offering her some, and she puts her fingers together indicating a small amount.

I've only been gone about two weeks, but it seems like a lifetime. Montana's grown on me, though more like a fungus than anything else. But Chance and Miles aren't the total assholes I expected them to be. They're loyal and protective, smart and... well, annoying.

Then there's Carly. I didn't expect her. Never in a million years. The three people eating dinner with me are my only family. But Carly, who's a time zone away, is who I crave to be with. And it isn't just the sex. Her perfect body. How I get lost in her. How I make her give me everything.

No. It's her. All of her. Cautious, scarred, skittish, brave, passionate. Fierce.

"Please call me Diana," Mom says. "I admit, seeing you three together is something. I heard there were two other Bridger boys, but you're men now."

"We don't get along all that well," Chance admits. He puts down his chicken leg and wipes his hands on his paper napkin.

Mom's house is the same one she's had since I was a kid.

Fortunately, it's a rancher, so there aren't any stairs for her to climb. It hasn't been updated in a while so the wallpaper in the kitchen is yellow and so are the cabinets. To me, it's home, even though I moved out when I was twenty-two.

Chance is a billionaire. While the money may not have been in his name, he grew up on a huge ranch in Montana, never wanting for anything. I mean, he has a fucking plane! Yeah, so do I, but his is a freaking jet. Yet he's here eating dinner in Mom's simple house, getting seconds and thirds like he fits in.

Maybe he does.

Maybe I'm too hard on him. How would I feel if all of a sudden I had to split my father's billions with two brothers I never even met? If I had to wait a fucking year to get it, and said brothers knew shit about anything related to ranching?

Mom's dark hair matches mine, although a few grays are peeking through her long hairstyle. I can tell the meds are working because she's not stiff and she's eating well. Thank God for that.

She laughs. "Brothers never get along. Fighting about chores and girls."

Miles laughs. "Girls? That's Austin's deal."

"Girls?" Mom glances my way. I can tell she's focusing on the plural word usage.

"Girl. Singular. And she's a woman, fully grown."

Those lush curves I had in my hands—and mouth—proved that.

"Carly," Miles adds. "She works at the ranch."

I glare at Miles. "Want to tell her everything for me?"

He holds up his hands in surrender. "You can tell her about Carly. All I can speak to are the chores. I'm from New York and this morning I dismantled a beaver dam."

Mom drops her mouth open.

"That was a first for me," Miles continues. "So's being here with you."

"Jonathan divorced both your mothers?" Mom asks.

Chance and Miles nod in freaky synchrony.

"I'd like to meet them. I'm sure we'd have fun together."

"Billionaire Wives Club?" I ask, even though she didn't see billions. Ever.

She raises her hands in the air. "Perfect idea! Then you three are the—"

"Billion Heirs," I say.

Her smile slips. "I hope money is all that you inherit from your father."

I glance at Chance and then Miles.

"Although from just a short time meeting you two, I know that's not the case."

Chance takes a sip of his iced tea. "What do you mean?"

His voice is calm and even, not showing a hint of the anger he's shown me since I arrived. Then again, she didn't ignore his warning and sleep with a woman he's protecting.

"You lived with your father until he died. Yes?" she asks.

Chance nods. "But we weren't close."

I can tell there's more to that sentence, but he's being diplomatic. I'm not sure if it's out of kindness to my mom, or if he's minimizing his past because it sucks.

"He divorced my mother when she was pregnant with me," Miles tells her. "I understand that's the same with you."

Mom nods. "Yes, but..." She flicks her dark gaze at Chance and then looks away.

"Nothing you can say will hurt my feelings when it comes to my father," Chance says. "*Our* father."

She clears her throat. "We were both fairly young when we met. Me more than Jonathan. And like you said, Miles, he divorced me when I told him I was having a baby."

I reach out and set my hand on her forearm. Give her a smile.

She offers one back and takes a shaky breath.

"He was sweet to me while we dated. And a short time

into our marriage. Then he changed. Became mean. He didn't want a child and was so angry at me for getting pregnant, as if it doesn't take two people to make it happen." She swallows. "I also learned that he was having affairs."

Holy shit.

"He slept around?" I ask, although I shouldn't be too surprised.

She nods. "Very young women. I was twenty-two, but he liked them even younger."

"He did," Chance agrees. "He told me I was a mistake. Never let me forget that. That the women he married messed everything up by getting pregnant."

"Jesus, didn't he know about condoms?" Miles asks, although we all know the answer to that. He glances at Mom and sheepishly adds, "Sorry, ma'am."

She waves him off. "It's been thirty-five years. I got the best thing out of the marriage right here. I'm sure your mothers think the same."

Silence for a moment, until Chance speaks.

"He never married again, obviously. He didn't date, either. I'd say he fucked his way through Western Montana. I didn't keep track, but I agree that he had a thing for...barely legal women."

Chance runs a hand over his face and my stomach sours. A rich old guy flashing his cash—and his dick—

would definitely interest some women, no matter how young.

"Then why did you stay? I mean, you could have just up and left," Miles says.

Chance pokes at a piece of chicken on the platter. "I never loved my dad. He was pretty much always an asshole. But I loved the land. Still do. Dealing with him was the sacrifice I made for what I wanted out of life."

"To be a cowboy," I say.

"Rancher."

"If the big hat fits..." Miles points to the Stetson sitting on the counter.

Chance shrugs.

"Well, don't let that man put you off your food," Mom gestures to the bowls and platters before us. "Tell me about Carly."

"I can do that," I tell her, "but we should talk about Greg and our plan for getting the plane back in the air."

I'd rather talk about the gorgeous brunette, but we're here in Seattle for a reason. We only have a week and need to get on it. Fast.

"The way we figure, Austin will fly the routes," Miles says. "I'll work with you, Diana, on putting out a job posting and getting someone hired. Meanwhile, Chance can go beat the shi— crap out of this Greg guy."

That lifts the mood and we all laugh.

"Sounds like a plan," Mom says. "I especially like the part where Chance kicks Greg's butt. I can call up the applicants we didn't accept when we hired Greg. Should hopefully only be some phone calls. And maybe some background checks. Eat up, boys. We've got work to do."

 ARLY

THE NIGHT BEFORE, I slept fitfully. The conversation with my father was stuck in my head because... God.

He's most likely the reason you were taken.

At dinner, I forced two tacos down to avoid my mother asking why I wasn't eating. They sat in my belly giving me heartburn as I lay in bed, wishing for Austin's strong arms around me. To tell me everything is going to be okay. That I'm safe.

Unfortunately, he didn't call last night, even after he texted me to let me know he landed safely. We're not anything but lovers, although he did say I was his. Still, it's been a matter of days and I shouldn't be attached. Shouldn't rely on him even though my pussy is sore and a constant reminder of what we did together.

Deep down, I know Austin never even met his father. But I'm trying not to concern myself with the fact... and the fact that my father believes—and may well be right—that Jonathan Bridger was involved in my abduction.

That the father of the man I'm falling for was evil.

I can't change it. I can only move forward. The fact that Jonathan Bridger is dead gives me comfort. Morbid? Yes. But I lived through hell. I'm glad I didn't know about this until after he was six feet under. Dad's voice became so robotic in the den as he told me he believed the elder Bridger had something to do with my abduction, and he —Dad—was looking into every kind of legal remedy available to us. That the FBI contact was also following through. It made Dad panic. Heck, I was a little freaked by it, but I know that it has nothing to do with Austin and Miles. Chance, too, even though he lived on the ranch with his dad. His anger is justified and if it's confirmed, I'll be so upset, too. Until then, I have to keep looking forward.

No wonder he's so upset about me working at Bridger Ranch. But I'm not in danger and I can't be taken again. Jonathan Bridger's dead. Derek Wolfe's dead. Maybe working at the ranch is actually the best way for me to move on, or is it just cruel to do so? To work the land of the man who possibly helped steal three years of my life... who almost destroyed me?

I don't know the answer yet. I'm overwhelmed and confused. Pulled in two directions. Maybe being here is proof that I survived. That I won't let him win, even from the grave. Inwardly, I smirk. Maybe he's rolling over in his casket right now with me taking care of his animals and sleeping with his son.

Maybe.

All I know is for today, I'm okay. I'm moving on. Doing the best I can and trying not to shift in my seat, my pussy achy from Austin's thorough attention.

I'm in the passenger side of an ATV while Lexie drives across the terrain to Shipp's Creek. It's bumpy and dusty and the sun is beating down on us. I put on a hat to shield my face from the strong rays, but I have to smile. ATVs are fun.

"The guys broke up the dam yesterday before they flew out," Lexie says, steering around a rock sticking out of the dirt. "So we need to scout the area for beavers and other wildlife that could be affected by the removal. If we find any, we'll need to alert the Fish and Wildlife Service and have them relocated."

"Well, obviously the beavers will be affected," I say. I watched a documentary once about how beavers are environmental engineers, changing the natural landscape unlike any other animal.

"Not necessarily." Lexie takes a swallow from the water bottle she brought along as she expertly steers with one hand. "The dam was old, as I understand it. We haven't had any beavers on any of the creeks through Bridger land for the last few years."

"Any interaction with grizzlies?"

She shakes her head. "Not on our ranch. They're still farther north. I saw some when hiking in Glacier National Park last summer. They're gorgeous but dangerous—and also endangered. Sometimes I don't understand why the most beautiful things seem to be fading out of existence."

Her words strike me hard, right in the gut.

Fading out of existence.

For so long, while I was on the island, I felt like I was fading out of existence. Even after I was rescued, during that first year of intensive therapy, I felt like a shadow. Like a two-dimensional cutout of Carly Vance.

Like an endangered species.

But not anymore.

I can't let myself go there anymore. Working here on the ranch with Lexie helps a lot.

Being with Austin helps even more.

It's ironic though, that I love the ranch of the man who may have been involved in my kidnapping.

Lexie pulls the ATV to a stop. "Here we are. From the directions Chance gave, we'll walk the rest of the way following the creek. The site of the dam is about a half mile up." She points as she slings a backpack over her shoulder.

I nod and follow. Together we trudge, following the creek, until we find the remains of the dam. Rotting logs and rocks are strewn along the bank on both sides. I could imagine the three brothers wet and muddy working on this project.

Lexie steps into the creek, the water sloshing around her ankles now that it's no longer blocked.

"What do you want me to do?" I ask.

"Walk along the bank. I doubt there are any beavers, but look for scat. It looks kind of like wood chips. If you find any, that means we'll need to have the animals relocated so they don't rebuild."

"Sounds reasonable." Very reasonable. I don't want my father to have any further reason to be upset with the Bridgers, though they can hardly be blamed for what a beaver does.

"Our responsibility is to notify the Fish and Wildlife Service and the Montana Fish and Wildlife Commission if we find evidence of them," Lexie continues. "They'll take care of the relocation."

I shake my head. "We didn't learn about beavers in the

first year of vet school."

"Vet school won't teach you about natural habitat. You'll learn more about that by doing hands-on work on the ranch than you'd learn at school." Lexie wipes a hand across her sweaty brow. "Trust me."

Yeah. Easy for her to say. She got to finish school. I turn and begin scouting for beaver scat.

This is what I'm doing today. Searching for shit. I want to laugh, but the other option was shoveling it back at the stable.

I remove my gloves for a moment to check my phone. Surely Austin has texted by now. I pull the phone from my pocket and—

No service. I sigh as I glance around. Open fields, a creek that twists and meanders through them. Cottonwood trees loom in shady patches over the water. It's a beautiful spot, but not as pretty as the spring I showed Austin. Which only makes me think of what we did there together. My whole body warms—and not from the sun.

I continue my walk along the bank of the creek. No evidence of beavers so far, but I spot a ground squirrel and a circling raptor. I walk away from the water, checking secluded areas.

Still nothing.

I return to Lexie. "Rabbit pellets but no beaver scat. I'll check the other side. Have you found anything?"

She turns and glances up at me from mid-creek. "Just one poor trout that got tangled in the brush. Otherwise, the water is flowing smoothly through the area where they broke up the dam. The guys did a good job, but I expected no less. Chance Bridger knows this land better than anyone. He's got a sixth sense about everything that lives here, both his animals and the wildlife. It's pretty amazing. He's a born rancher."

"Seems his brothers aren't," I say.

She smiles. "They'll learn. Bridger blood. Jonathan Bridger may have been an ass, but he knew his stuff. Chance learned from the best."

Interesting. Obviously she met Jonathan Bridger with him being her boss and all. Still, the guy was literally infamous. He married and discarded three wives after they each gave him a son.

He also somehow turned the biggest ranch in Montana into a billion-dollar enterprise.

But couldn't be bothered to care for his wives or sons.

And now, according to my father...

He might have been behind my abduction.

I shake my head to clear the thoughts. I have a job to do, and that is to cross the creek and keep looking for beaver shit. Dare to dream.

I trudge through the water and as I wade farther it

deepens where the original creek bed probably mean-dered pre-dam. I get wet up to my thighs.

When I finally hit the other side, my jeans are clinging to me and mud has caked through my boots. "Jeez," I mutter. I'd better find some beaver poop to make this all worthwhile.

One more step, and I'll be back on solid—

I stumble over a rock or log underneath the water.

"You okay?" Lexie asks from the other side.

"Yeah. Just tripped over something."

"Probably just a big rock," she calls.

"Right."

Except it doesn't feel like a rock. It feels kind of... pliable. That's the last I think of it, though, because the beaver poop awaits. I step out of the water. The creek goes down a little when I step out, my body having displaced it. I cast a glance toward where I stumbled, and—

My legs turn to jelly, but I catch myself before I lose my footing.

"Oh shit," I breathe. My heart skips a beat and my skin chills as I go numb.

It's not a rock.

It's gray, and gnarly, and...

It's looking straight at me with translucent, sightless eyes.

My gut clenches and I hold back the puke that threatens to erupt.

It's a head. A human head, most likely attached to a body.

A *very* dead body, what is left of it.

I open my mouth to yell for Lexie, but nothing comes out.

My legs give way, and I tumble to the muddy ground, my vision blurring.

 USTIN

"THAT'S IT," I say to Miles and Chance as we walk toward Sea-Air headquarters, located at their harbor base. Their dock is longer than where we land, with buoys and lights to warn boaters of landing planes. "According to Mom, Greg is manning this morning's flight to Vancouver Island."

Chance is walking a step behind me. "So he's not flying for Lovering?"

I huff. "Hell, no. Mom fired his ass. *I'll* be flying for Lovering."

"For this week." From Miles. "What about after that?"

I have no idea what will happen after that if we don't find another replacement, and they both know it, so I don't bother replying. Especially once the seaplane with the Sea-Air logo floats carefully to the dock. Someone's there to tie it off, which reminds me I need to have a little chat with Ed, our dock man.

"That him?" Chance asks, his voice loud over the noise of the engine.

"I assume so," I say. "I've never met the traitorous bastard." I walk toward the plane as it stops, my two giant brothers in tow. The sway of the dock feels familiar beneath my feet.

The pilot—Greg, I assume—removes his headphones and deplanes. He's tall but thin, and his jeans look like they're about to fall off his ass. His stringy hair is pulled into a manbun. How the fuck does he get the headphones on over that thing?

"You Greg?" I ask.

"Guilty," he says, looking between the three of us as he steps up from the running board and onto the dock. "You my passengers?"

"Fuck, no," I say. "I'm Austin Bridger. Diana Lovering's son, and these are my brothers. We're here to get Lovering's routes back."

Greg backs away slightly. "Hey, I don't want any trouble."

"Then give Diana her flights back," Miles said. "We'll be happy to leave quietly with you in one piece."

Chance has always come across as the more aggressive brother, but I have a feeling Miles has been in a fight or two and I have no doubt he can hold his own.

"What the fuck?" Greg asks, scratching his wild hair. "I thought Diana only had one son, and he's in Montana or something."

"Diana has one son," I say. "Me. But Miles and Chance are my brothers."

"What kind of asshole are you?" Chance demands. "Taking advantage of a woman who has MS? Who's worked her ass off her whole life to build up her business? Who does that kind of shit?"

Chance listened when I explained my background. About my mom.

"Look, man." Greg backs away, hands up, as if they will protect him.

Can't blame the guy. Chance is the size of a Mack truck and I know what his punch feels like.

"Like I said, I don't want any trouble," he repeats. "I'm just the pilot."

"Yeah, you're a fucking broken record. Then you shouldn't have taken our routes."

"Take it up with my boss, man." He points toward the end of the doc where the small Sea-Air office is.

"Oh, don't worry," I say. "We'll take it up with him. After this."

I step up and punch him in the face.

Unfortunately, he doesn't fall to the dock or into the water, but he rocks back. "Ow, shit. What the fuck, man?" His hand goes to his clearly broken nose, blood seeping between his fingers and down his chin.

"You fuck with Lovering Air, you fuck with my mother, you get me." I snarl. "That punch was for her."

Greg's right. He's just the pilot. While he's smart enough to get his license, he's a fucking patsy for doing what his boss says, including being a slimy shit and stealing routes as part of his job. He could've manned up and told the fucker no and he'd have had a legit job at Lovering.

I turn and head down the dock to the office and deal with his boss—the one who wanted to fuck us over.

I stalk off, my brothers following, ready to deal with the next guy who fucked with what's mine.

"Can I punch the next one?" Chance asks.

I swear I hear him crack his knuckles behind me.

I have to laugh. It's pretty cool to have brothers. I might soon have billions, but not everything is solved by tossing money around. A few punches might need to be thrown, too. Even after a short time, Chance and Miles have my back. For once, I don't feel alone in all the shit that's piled up.

———

"I'LL BE GODDAMNED!" Miles laughs up a storm as we drive back to Mom's. "Chance, buddy, I have new respect for you."

"You didn't respect me before I threatened the owner?" Chance asks innocently, glancing over at Miles who's in the back seat.

"That fucking helped," I say.

We stormed into the office and for some reason, Chance had more anger toward the asshole than I did, which was a metric shit-ton. He didn't give the guy much choice between giving back the routes that had been stolen or eating through a straw for the next few months. The shit-head agreed to call the clients he'd poached and tell them he'd solely been filling in. That he'd continue to do so until Lovering Air has a replacement pilot. *So generous* of him.

Chance was scary as fuck. For once, I'm glad his anger was aimed at someone else.

"You didn't exactly welcome us into your life with open arms," I remind him.

"I—"

"Brother, it's okay. Especially after that." I clap him on the shoulder while I man the steering wheel with the other hand.

I'm driving us back to the Lovering office because I need to fly today's routes while Mom and Miles work on finding a new pilot.

"You're the one who punched a guy back there. I only threatened," Chance says. "Though I have to admit I'd have liked to remove the teeth from that smug little mouth of his."

"Your threat was enough," I say. "Thanks. As for before, when we first showed up at the ranch. I know you had your reasons for hating me."

"Us," Miles adds.

"I get it," I continue. "And you've more than made up for it today. One look at you and that Sea-Air fucker nearly pissed himself."

"I'm pretty sure he actually did," Miles says from the back.

"Yeah, well..." Chance looks straight ahead out the front windshield. "I owe you. For that night at the Dusty Rose. I shouldn't have hit you."

"Damn right you shouldn't have. I'd never disrespect a woman. Especially Carly. But we're good."

"I don't like people taking advantage," he replies.

I'm seeing Chance much differently now. He protected

Carly, and today he protected my mom and me, our business. Where does this protective streak come from? From his—*our*—father? I doubt it. Chance has a story, but already I know he'll only tell it in his own time. Maybe he'll share it over the next year.

"I respect that you care so much about Carly," I say, "but I'd never do that to any woman. And Carly... She's something special for sure."

My mind fills with visions of Carly in that hidden spring. Of her in my arms. Bare except for her panties. Her breasts filling my palms. Her tongue tangling with mine. Of the night in my bed. Of me taking her roughly against my bedroom wall.

I shift in my seat at the sudden tightness of my jeans.

"So what about the two of you, then?" Chance asks. "What are you going to do?"

"What do you mean?" Everything between Carly and me plays in my mind like a movie. How she looks to me with those trusting green eyes. How she closes them when I'm deep inside her, pushing her into another orgasm. How her fragility isn't really fragility at all, but a fierce determination to heal, to grow, to empower herself.

What about the two of us?

I'm damned near in love with her because while it feels good to be back here in Seattle, I miss Carly something fucking fierce. All I want to do is get back to her. Get back *in* her.

Damn.

"The mayor hates us, Austin," Chance says. "You saw him. What if he finds out the government is trying to freeze our funds?" He sighs. "His anger's been aimed at only me since our father died. Now that you two are on the scene, he's happily spread his dislike to you two. Except, Jesus, Austin. Falling for his *daughter?* Fuck, it's a wonder you're not behind bars on some trumped up charge or dead. Carly's—"

"A grown woman," I finish for him. "An intelligent twenty-seven-year-old woman who's trying to take back her life, and she's succeeding. If I can be a part of that, I want to be."

"You sure she's ready?" he says.

"That's her decision, and—"

My cell rings and I answer it by accepting the call on the car's display since I have it synced.

"Mom, you'll be happy to hear—"

"Honey"—she cuts me off, her voice tinged with anxiety—"I'm headed to the hospital."

"What?" I slam on the brakes and pull to the side of the road.

The car behind me honks, angry by my quick action, but I ignore it.

Chance offers me a concerned look but stays silent.

"What's wrong?"

"I was lightheaded. Blood pressure, I think. I fell in the bathroom."

Fuck. Her master bath is small which means lots of hard edges to strike.

"How are you hurt?" I clench the wheel, wishing I could take this burden from her.

"They're worried I broke my hip. I'm with nice para-medics and they're taking care of me."

Shit. She was alone and had to call 9-1-1. And a broken hip? That will be a huge setback in so many ways. She seems calm enough, but she may already be on pain meds —and if she is, that means it's bad. Possible surgery, rehab. Her house is one floor but not the best for a wheelchair. She'll need help. That means me or money for an aide.

"Which hospital?" I ask, not jumping too far ahead.

"St. Anne's."

"We'll meet you there."

Before I can even end the call, I get another. Carly's name replaces Mom's on the display.

"All right, sweetheart," Mom says, hanging up.

I haven't spoken to Carly since we left and this isn't the best time. I'm aching to hear her voice, to listen to her talk about the animals on the ranch. Hell, I'll even listen to talk of shoveling manure if she's the one doing it.

Except I can't do it now. Not on the way to the ER and not with Chance and Miles in the car.

Looking over my shoulder, I pull a U-turn and floor it toward the hospital closest to Mom's house. It's ten minutes away, but at least I know she's breathing and headed to St. Anne's.

"Don't you want to get that?" Miles leans forward and sets his forearms on the two front seats.

I glance at Carly's name, but then it disappears. She ended the call.

"I'll get back to her." *When I know my mom is stable and things aren't a total shitshow.*

Except it rings again. I grit my teeth and press the accept button. No way can I blow Carly off twice in a row. It felt wrong the first time.

"Hey, baby. Can I call you back? Now's not—"

"No." Her voice is breathy through the speaker. "Oh my God, Austin. You won't... I mean..." Her voice is breathy.

My heart is already on overdrive and now it's full out in a stampede. Mom. And now Carly. She's freaked.

"Breathe and tell me what's wrong."

Chance's cell rings and he pulls it from his pocket, puts it to his ear.

"At the dam. I... I... I found a..."

"It's okay, baby. Just tell me."

Her breath comes in rapid puffs through the phone. "A... A dead body."

"What the fuck?" Miles murmurs.

I don't know who Chance is talking to, but his face goes hard, his jaw clenches, and he looks at me and nods. He's getting the same info from someone else. A foreman maybe? Hell, it could even be Mayor Vance for all I fucking know.

For the second time in a few minutes, I slam on the brakes and pull off the road.

"There's a dead body on the ranch," Chance confirms. "At the creek. We have to get back. Together. Now."

"My mom's headed to the ER," I say. "I have routes to fly."

"Your girl needs you," Miles says.

"So does my mom," I snap.

I'm being pulled in multiple directions, and I don't know what to do. I don't fucking know where to even go.

"Austin—" Carly practically sobs.

Her cries tear at my chest like invisible knives.

I run a hand over my face. Fuck. What the hell am I going to do?

 ARLY

I'M EXHAUSTED. And caked in dry mud.

Lexie's at the police station with me and we've been questioned for hours. I'm not sure how many more ways we can say we know nothing about the body I found.

After the two of us totally freaked, we stood on the bank of the creek and pulled our shit together. We decided we'd both ride back to the ranch to get help. Neither of us wanted to remain behind with the body. It wasn't going anywhere.

So we took the ATV to the stable, which happened to

be the closest building, and called the police. Only when they arrived did we lead them back, a few of the ranch hands joining us. Photos were taken and then the body loaded into a body bag for a trip to the morgue.

"You said the Bridgers were at the dam yesterday?" Chief Bryant asks.

He's close in age to my parents and nearing retirement. Not much happens in Bayfield, so a dead body is definitely news. I'm not sure if he knows what to even do about it. The last big thing to happen in town was...*me*. My kidnapping.

"Yes." Lexie runs a hand over her hair that's snarled and wispy from our hasty trips back and forth from the creek.

"My father was upset about the dam blocking other neighbors' access to water. The men dismantled the dam yesterday at his... suggestion."

"Now they're out of state," the sheriff says. "All three of them. That's convenient."

"I don't think they're on the run, sir." I try to keep the man focused. It's not my place to mention the will and the weird requirements that go along with it. "Austin had some issues with his family business."

"I thought the ranch *was* family business," Bryant counters.

"Austin is new to Bayfield, as you know. He has run a

seaplane company with his mother for years. I'm not sure though what this has to do with the body."

Sheriff Bryant purses his lips.

I swallow. "You don't think he has anything to do with this, do you?"

"Well—"

"Austin's only been in Bayfield for what... two weeks? I'm not an expert on dead bodies—"

"Then you don't need to continue."

"I did trip over him, Sheriff. I got quite the look at the man. The body. He... *it's* been there a while."

Lexie takes my hand in hers and gives it a squeeze. "Can we go, Sheriff? You know where to find both of us if you have more questions."

Bryant pauses, rubs his jawline and then nods.

Thank God.

We stand and walk out of his office.

My parents hop to their feet and head toward me. I'm not sure how long they've been here, but the vintage vinyl chairs in the small lobby can't be comfortable.

My mom hugs me as my father looks me over.

"Are you all right, honey?" she asks.

I nod and remember my manners.

"Mom, Dad, this is Dr. Lexie Davis, the vet at the ranch."

Dad frowns a bit but then nods. "If you'd quit like I wanted, you wouldn't have found a damned body."

"If you hadn't forced the dam to be broken apart, I wouldn't have found a damned body," I reply.

"Carly," my mom gently scolds.

"Mom, I'm sorry, but you can't blame this situation on the fact that I want to keep working at the ranch. Or on the Bridger brothers because it was on their property. They only went to the dam because Dad was furious about the water rights."

Lexie hasn't said one word, and I don't blame her.

"A dead body was found on Bridger land," Dad says. "That's bad enough. You need to quit."

I solidify my stance, wishing I made a more imposing presence. "No, I don't. I won't."

Dad's jaw tenses. "Because of your...fling with Austin Bridger?"

Fling? What I have with Austin isn't a fling. It's... I don't know exactly, but it's more than what my father is assuming. But as much as Austin means to me, there's another reason I won't quit. One I desperately need my father to understand.

"No, because as I've told you over and over, I love my job. It makes me happy. Isn't that what's important?"

"You found a *dead body*." Dad's tone is final.

As far as he's concerned, the matter is resolved.

But his concern isn't the issue. Mine is. And I'm not quitting.

While I'm trying to figure out a way to tell my father this—

I drop my jaw and widen my eyes.

The Bridger boys come rushing in the station's front doors—Chance first, followed by Miles, and then...Austin.

The walls—the ones I've had in place around my emotions since I first realized what I stumbled over in the creek wasn't a rock—come crumbling down when I see Austin. I run to him. Miles steps out of the way before I knock him over.

Austin holds out his hand. I take it and walk into him, and he wraps his arms around me. I bury my face in his chest and breathe him in—all masculine spice and musk, all power and perfection.

His strength gives me strength of my own, and I revel in his hold.

Tears start to fall. I can't help them.

"Carly." My father's voice.

Austin drops a kiss on the top of my head and then murmurs, "You okay, baby?"

I nod.

I shake my head.

I shrug.

I don't know what I am...except in love. In complete and total love with Austin Bridger. I called him hours ago when he was far away. Now he's here.

"She all done here, Sheriff?" Austin asks.

"For now. I'll want to talk to the three of you as well."

"Tomorrow," Chance replies with enough authority that Bryant doesn't say more.

"You're coming with us, Carly," my father says.

I turn my head to look at my parents, but I stay in Austin's tight embrace.

Austin came for me. He's here in the station, back in Montana, because of me. I'm not sure what he's learned about the dead body other than what I told him on the frantic phone call. Chance has no doubt been given updates, but still... Austin didn't question me first and hug me after.

No. Comfort first. Comfort from Austin.

And my God, I need it. I used to—and still do—get it from my parents, but this is different. It's more. Even after knowing this man for such a short time.

He said I was his.

He's right.

I'm his. I'm Austin's. Forever, if he'll have me.

I gather my strength, pull back slightly from Austin's

hold, and meet my father's gaze. "No, Daddy. I'm going with Austin."

Austin doesn't say anything, just gives my hip a squeeze.

My mom sniffles. "Rick..."

"This only adds to what I told you about Jonathan Bridger," Dad says. "About that family. The ranch."

"Don't make her choose," Mom tugs on Dad's arm.

"We raised her better than this, Darla. To be smarter."

Tears fall and I let them. I'm not heartbroken about my father's words. He has his ideas about Austin based solely on his paternity, and he's made his feelings clear. What saddens me is that I see Dad differently now. No longer is he the rock who always shields me, protects me, and who I listen to without question. Now he's a real person. A real person with flaws—cracks in his perfect facade.

I swallow hard. "You raised me well, Daddy. You raised me to be strong and to be able to make my own choices. I love you for it. I love you both. But I'm going with Austin."

Everyone's watching. Chance and Miles. Lexie. The sheriff.

"Ready?" Austin murmurs.

I nod.

"I'll take care of her, Mr. Vance. I swear it." Austin turns and leads me out the door.

The air's cooler now, the sun low in the western sky.

"Come on. Let's go home."

I shake my head and he stops in the parking lot. Looking down, he cups my face in his big palms.

"What is it?" he asks. His eyes are dark and fathomless. I want to get lost in them. In him.

"I... I don't have a home."

The realization aches in my whole body. I'm twenty-seven and coasting through life in my childhood, pale yellow bedroom. No house of my own. Not even a rental apartment.

He leans down, swipes his lips over mine. "I don't have one either. But, baby, I think I just realized that home isn't a place. It's a person. And my home's with you."

"But Seattle... Your mom..."

Austin sighs. "I have to figure everything out, but my brothers..." He smiles. "It still seems weird to call them that, but my brothers helped me get Mom's routes back. She fell earlier and she's in the hospital with a broken hip—"

I gasp.

"But her prognosis is excellent," he continues.

"No wonder you nearly didn't take my call. I'm so sorry, Austin."

"It took me about a second to realize you're my first

priority," he says. "Mom is right up there, in second place, and Chance and Miles and the ranch in third. But you, Carly Vance, are everything to me."

"Oh, Austin." I kiss his cheek. "Yes. Please take me home."

 USTIN

I USED to think I wouldn't do laundry for any woman but my mother. It's a pain in the ass, and one of the household chores I hate most.

But here I am, unloading the Bridger washing machine because the housekeeper is busy making dinner. Carly doesn't have any clothes here, so I put her dirty stuff through a cycle while she showers.

I thought about joining her, but we both decided she needed to relax alone for a bit. We'll have plenty of time for lovemaking later. Once I get her beneath me, I'm not letting her up for a good long while.

Maybe not even a lifetime.

I pull her damp clothes out of the washing machine and throw them into the dryer, and then I join her out on the deck. Alone. I don't know where my brothers are, but I'm thankful they've made themselves scarce.

She's sitting in an Adirondack chair wearing only one of my large T-shirts. Her hair hangs in wet waves around her shoulders, and her skin is scrubbed clean.

I've been thinking while she showered—thinking about something I'd rather forget.

But I can't.

I called my mom and she's doing fine. In fact, she begged me not to return to Seattle, not to give up my inheritance, for her. She has friends who are checking in, and she'll be in rehab soon with all her needs met.

But God, the guilt...

My mom was always the one constant in my life, and now I can't be the constant in hers.

"Don't you dare feel guilty," she said to me on the phone. "This is your time to shine, Austin. I'll be okay. The business will be okay because I have a shortlist of pilots I can call who wanted the job. I'm sure one of them will take it. So don't even think about giving up on your inheritance or more importantly, your chance to fall in love. I want grandkids."

Her words still hang in my mind.

My mom means so much to me, and I'd feel awful if we were at odds.

So I have to have a tough conversation with Carly.

As much as I loved that she came to me at the station, that she left with me instead of her family, she's in the middle. Pulled in two directions. Her family is important to her as much as my mom is to me. I can't have them be at odds. I won't.

I'd love to have her here with me—as much as I yearn for her constantly—but she needs to go home. She needs to make things right with her father. I won't be able to have her completely happy if she has to choose. I don't want her to do so.

With my mom in the hospital, I recognize the feeling of having to choose between who you love and who to be with. But Mom and I aren't fighting.

Carly smiles and looks up when I settle in the chair beside her. It's dark out, but soft lights are built into the underside of the deck's railing. I can see her clearly, but nothing beyond the golden glow.

"Hey, baby." I take her hand. "How are you feeling?"

"I'm okay." She sighs, playing with the bottom of my t-shirt that rests mid-thigh. I feel like a caveman seeing her wearing it and I wonder what she has on beneath. If anything. "Really. I've been through much worse."

I tense, as I do whenever I think about what she experienced. But I, like she, must come to terms with it and move forward. As much as it pains me to know what she's been through, if she can move on, I must as well.

I draw in a deep breath. "You have, and you're amazing."

She shrugs her slim shoulders. "It's nothing anyone else couldn't do."

"Give yourself credit," I tell her. *Nothing anyone else couldn't do?* Survive being kidnapped and shipped to a sinister island where she was used and abused? "You have so much inner fortitude. You deserve everything good. Which is why—"

"I have to go home." Her voice is soft. Her gaze drops to my chest. Nervous, or shy. Or afraid.

I drop my mouth open. She was pondering the same thing as I was. "Baby?"

"I've been sitting out here thinking, Austin. I don't regret coming with you, and I'd do it again. I showed my parents what you mean to me, and that neither of them can control me. But..."

I smile, bring her hand to my lips and kiss her fingers. One after the other. "I understand. I was about to tell you the same thing."

She looks up and smiles weakly. "You're kidding, right?"

I shake my head. "I'm not. While you were in the

shower, I talked to my mom. She's going to have surgery on her hip, not a replacement, and she'll be in rehab for a month or so. The new meds for MS she's taking are working well, though, so that's good news."

"I'm glad to hear that," she says.

"Thanks, baby. I have a feeling she'll even have a pilot before the week's out. She's determined."

"I'm glad she wants to keep the business she started going."

I give her a small smile. "I think it's more about me being here with you."

She flushes even in the soft lighting.

"Anyway," I continue, because we're not ready for the kid convo yet, "you know how much my mom means to me, and I know your dad means the same to you. I'd be lost if Mom and I weren't on good terms, and I don't want that for you. I agree. You need to go home to work things out with your dad."

"I don't want to leave you." She turns her hand over and grasps my fingers.

"I know." With my free hand, I reach out and tuck her damp hair behind her ear. "I don't want you to leave, either, but we're both right. You need to talk to him. You'll feel much better when you do. I'm not going anywhere. I'll be here once you and your dad are good again. I won't put you in the middle. If this is going to be long term, which it is," I add, ensuring she still knows she's mine, "I don't want him hating me."

She rises. "I know."

"It'll be another half hour until your clothes are dry, though." I raise an eyebrow and give a sly smile. Thirty minutes isn't a long time, but I can be creative. "Any ideas what we can do until then?"

Before she answers, though, Chance opens the French door to the deck. "Dinner's on the table, you two."

"Rotten timing," I mutter, even though the scent of garlic wafts from the house and makes my stomach rumble.

Carly turns to me. "Are you hungry?"

"Not for food," I say.

She smiles, and damn, she's beautiful.

"I'm not sure I should join your brothers at the table wearing only this." She looks down at the T-shirt that hits her just above her knees.

"I don't like the idea of any man seeing you like this, but you're completely covered, and you look amazing. I promised your dad I'd take care of you, and that means feeding you."

"Believe it or not, I actually feel like I could eat. I haven't had anything since breakfast."

I'm not surprised. Once they found that body, the

sheriff kept her and Lexie busy all day. Besides, a dead body can turn anyone off the idea of eating.

"Let's go then." I open the door for her.

Chance and Miles are seated in the kitchen's breakfast nook, so Carly and I join them.

I inhale. Smells great, kind of like ginger. "What's on the menu?"

Chance takes a sip from his beer bottle. "Pork stir fry. One of my favorites. Sit on down, both of you. There's plenty."

"What do you want to drink?" I ask Carly.

"Just ice water, please."

I take our two glasses from the already-set table and fill them with ice and water from the fridge. Meals are casual here, even though the housekeeper prepares them for us. We serve ourselves, which is fine with me.

"How are you feeling, Carly?" Miles asks.

"I'm okay." She takes the plate Chance has filled for her with food. "But I'll be going home tonight."

"This bum kicking you out?" Chance glances at me as I sit down, setting our glasses by our plates.

I give him a stink eye. "Of course not."

"I'm joking, asswipe. Damn."

"It was kind of a mutual decision," Carly says, maybe to keep us from bickering. "I have to work things out with my dad."

Chance nods. "That reminds me. Miles and I were talking earlier, and I'm sure Austin will agree. We'd like to quitclaim your land back to your mom and dad."

"What's that?" Carly asks.

"A change of name on a property deed. In this case, giving your land back to your parents. A legal handoff."

"Can we do that?" I ask. I don't know much about the logistics and legalities of property.

Chance nods. "Yeah. I got on the horn with Shankle and he says it's an easy transaction, though he did try to talk me out of it."

"Why?" I ask.

"Because he was our father's attorney long before he was ours, and that bastard never would have transferred a damned piece of lint without some kind of consideration. Proof of him being shady by taking the Vance's land in the first place. But I made it clear that we'd be doing this one way or another. I figured we'd have to wait a year until the money's ours to give the portion that was shafted, but Shankle says we can do the paperwork portion now if we want to."

"You just want to give it to my dad?" Carly's eyes are wide.

"Yeah," Miles says with a decisive nod. "We don't need it. Have you seen the size of this place?" He waves his hand around the huge kitchen. "Besides, we don't want something that shouldn't be ours."

Carly shakes her head, but not in answer to Miles' question. "My dad won't take it. He'll think it's charity."

"We're just trying to make things right," Chance says. "The three of us aren't our father."

"I know that," she says. "I've always known that. It's why I'm going home. He'll understand eventually, and this gesture may help."

"I'll have the papers by tomorrow," Chance says, "if Austin here agrees."

"Of course, I agree." I trail my finger over Carly's forearm.

"It's settled, then." Chance shoves a forkful of food into his mouth.

Carly smiles at me.

And for that single moment, all is right in this fucked-up world, if I don't think of the mysterious dead body that was uncovered, my mom in the hospital, my woman's dad hating my guts, the EPA after us, and...

Yeah, never mind.

ARLY

AUSTIN STANDS at the door of my parents' house with me, holding both my hands in his. "You sure you don't want me to come in with you?" he asks.

"Yes and no," I reply. It's not the first time I've ever felt nervous walking into my own home. But in the past few days, I'm not who I used to be. It's laughable since I was gone for over three years. That changed me, definitely, but this time, it's my choice.

My decisions that are changing the course of my life. They aren't what my parents want, but what *I* do.

He lowers his head, presses his lips against mine. "I understand."

"I need to do this alone." I hold his hand, clinging to him in contrast to my words. "Although I would love it if you could come in with me. I mean, how else will he find out how awesome you are except by giving you a chance?"

"Yeah, well, he's not really interested in giving me a chance. At least not yet. How about you go solo tonight with them tonight? Baby steps."

He's probably right, but dad also has to give *me* a chance.

"He'll come around. My father is a good man, Austin. Unfortunately, you haven't seen the best side of him."

My mind wanders to what my father told me—that Jonathan Bridger may have had a hand in my abduction. That's huge. Crazy serious and will impact Austin and his brothers.

Except that's not something I can burden Austin with, at least not yet. Not until I find out whether it's true or not, and maybe not even then. Austin is *not* his father, and he shouldn't have to live with what his father may have done. Same goes for Miles and Chance.

That's what I need to get my own father to understand, even if I have to hit him over the head with it.

"Call me," he says. "Just let me know you're okay

tonight. I'll see you tomorrow. I'll try to come find you during lunch. Do you know where you'll be?"

"I'll check in at the vet's office around noon," I say. "Unless they call me back into town for more questioning about that body."

"I doubt they will" His mouth thins into a line. "You've told them everything."

Over dinner, I shared with all three Bridger men what Lexie and I were asked, what we answered.

"True enough." I stand on my tiptoes and wrap my arms around his neck. "Thank you. For everything."

It's late, but there are lights on in the house.

"All I did was wash your clothes, baby."

I kiss his lips lightly. "You did a lot more than that, and you know it. Thank you for coming home. For... for choosing me."

He trails a finger over my jawline, traces my lower lip. "Carly, there was no other choice."

I open my mouth to speak, when—

My mother opens the door. She hasn't changed for bed, still in tan pants and a blue top I know is her favorite. "Carly, it's you! I heard a car pull up."

"I'm sorry if we scared you."

She looks between me and Austin. "Are you back?"

"For now." I pull away from him. "Goodbye, Austin."

"Hello, Mrs. Vance," he says to Mom and then glances

down at me. Brushes his knuckles over my cheek. "Good night, Carly. Call me."

"I will."

He steps back and returns to the Bridger Ranch truck he used to bring me home.

I walk inside and stand in front of the glass door, watching Austin as he heads down the drive. My heart breaks just a little, seeing him leave me. I drop to my knees and give Ernie lots of loves when he nudges my leg with his nose. I missed my silly dog, and if I do end up moving out, he's coming with me.

"Where's Dad?" I ask, glancing up at Mom.

"Where do you think? In that darned den of his. Still looking for answers."

I sigh. "I think he needs to let it go, Mom. Especially the part about the Bridgers."

"I wish he would." Mom rubs her hands together. Clearly she has different opinions on the subject than Dad, probably staying quiet to keep the peace. Or maybe she hasn't, and it's put tension between them. Thus, the grumpy face.

"I can't live my life afraid of my own shadow," I say. "The man's dead, so it's not like anything will ever come of it. I have to let it go, and so does he."

She twines her fingers. "But he's convinced that—"

I stand and come close, pull her fingers apart and give

her hand a squeeze. "I know. He told me. The whole town knows Jonathan Bridger was no saint. Maybe he truly was that evil. I mean, I just found a dead body on his land."

Her lips thin and she goes pale. "Which is why your father's concerned. Who knows what else is happening on that land?"

Maybe Mom's concerned too.

"But Jonathan Bridger is *dead*, Mom. The land belongs to his sons now, and they're good men, all three of them."

"You hardly know them."

I shake my head. "That's not true, and you know it. Chance and I went to school together. I've known him since I was a kid. We didn't hang out in the same circles, but he's a good guy. He was the one who bullied the bullies. I'm sure you've seen him around town a time or ten. People might talk about the elder Bridger, but Chance? I only hear good things. And Miles is funny and nice. And Austin..."

"Austin," my mom echoes, her eyes brightening. "What about Austin?"

"I'm having feelings for him, Mom. Feelings I didn't think I'd ever have again. It's scary, but it's also wonderful. I don't want it to stop. I'm not ending things with him just because Dad had issues in the past. Austin wasn't even here." I sigh. "I want to make things right with Dad, with you both, but I can't give Austin up."

Mom lets her hands drop to her sides. "It about killed your father when you went home with Austin this afternoon instead of with us."

Probably hurt her, too.

"I know it did, and that's why I'm back. Part of the reason, anyway. I do need to make things right with Daddy. And you. You know how much you both mean to me."

"Sweetheart, I don't think you understand the guilt your father feels. The guilt we both feel."

I frown. "What for?"

Her mouth opens for a second in stunned silence. "How can you even ask me that? For not protecting you."

"Protecting me? You mean from being taken?"

Her eyes well with tears, but she blinks them back.

"I was twenty-two years old," I say. "I wasn't at home. I was up at Millie's, out in public. Everyone in town eats there. I wasn't on a dangerous street corner in a big city. No one imagined something like that could happen here in Bayfield. You couldn't have stopped it."

She sighs. "Yes, we know that objectively. I've talked to a therapist about it. Your father won't."

I ache with the knowledge that they were so hurt by my disappearance. "Maybe he should."

She nods. "Yes, he probably should. But I wouldn't bring that up to him right now."

She has a point. One battle at a time. "All right. But I do need to talk to him."

Her smile is soft, as if I've eased her mind somewhat. "I know. Thank you for coming home. Thank you for seeing what's important."

"I do know what's important," I say, a little hurt that she thinks I don't feel she and my dad are important. But I've changed. Maybe quickly, but I have. I'm a grown woman and they're going to have to come to terms with my disappearance *and* me living my own life. Making my own decisions, even if they don't like them. "You and Dad are both very important to me. I love you. But Austin is also important to me. I won't be giving him up. No matter what. You were married to Dad before you were my age."

"I had you before your age," she added. I watch her brain process that, and then her lips form another straight line because I've pointed out something obvious. She had her own husband, house and child by the time she was my age. She did what she wanted, separate from her parents. "Go talk to him. He'll be glad to see you. Neither of us wants to make this hard on you. You've had enough difficulty to last a lifetime."

"It's true that I've had more difficulty than most, but we all need to move forward. That includes you, and that includes Dad. As long as he's letting these wounds fester, trying to figure out whether Jonathan Bridger had something to do with me being taken, he won't be able to move forward."

I don't wait for my mother to reply. I kiss her on the cheek and walk to the den. The door is cracked, but I knock anyway.

"What is it, Darla?"

I open the door. "It's me, Daddy."

He looks up, his eyes wide. "Carly."

"Yes. I came home."

He's behind his desk and his eyes fill with hope and determination at the sight of me. "Thank God you came to your senses."

I resist an eye roll. I'm here to work things out, not make things worse.

I walk inside his office and take a seat in front of the table. "I think we need to talk."

He firmly nods, his jaw set in his familiar stubborn tilt. "Absolutely, we do. No more Austin Bridger."

I shake my head. "Daddy, Austin is a good man. I've said this to you before. He's not his father. And neither are Miles and Chance."

"Do I need to remind you what happened just this morning?"

Was it just this morning? It's been a crazy, long day.

"Hardly. I haven't been able to get the image out of my mind."

"Good men don't normally have dead bodies on their property."

"The body was there for a long time, Daddy."

No one knew for sure how long ago the man died, but I overheard the coroner share an estimate of at least two months. "We don't even know if the man died in that spot, or if he was left on the Bridger property. It was found in a creek, so it could've come from anywhere, especially with those heavy spring rains we had. I know you remember all the flooded basements the town dealt with."

Dad harrumphs. As mayor, he certainly remembers all the chaos too much water brought to our small town.

At least he doesn't deny my words. My father may be angry and tense, but he's an intelligent man.

"The beaver dam is what kept him underwater all this time." A little shiver runs through me at the memory. "If you hadn't forced them to break it up, the body may never have been found. I'm sure the sheriff shared all this with you."

He looks down at his hands and nods. They are facts, not opinions, and I was the one who found the body, who knows as much, if not more, than him.

"Chance is going to go talk to the sheriff tomorrow," I add.

He looks up at me. "And the other two?"

"Unofficially, the death clearly predates their arrival at the ranch. The sheriff sees no reason to talk to them."

Dad's eyes flare. "He doesn't? Bryant grilled you and Dr. Davis for what seemed like hours."

"Because we found the body," I say. "They wanted information. They didn't think we had anything to do with it. Never once did they imply they thought we did anything wrong."

Dad shakes his head and looks down at some documents spread across his desk.

"I'm willing to stay home, Daddy," I tell him. "But my time here will be finite. Only until you and I work out our differences."

"You know what's necessary if that's what you want."

"Remember when we were at the sheriff's office today? When Mom asked you not to make me choose? Why would you want to do that? I'm twenty-seven, and you know I need to make a life for myself. I can't live at home forever."

"Not forever, Carly. Just until..."

"You can't even finish that sentence because you don't know the answer. You know I'm right. I told Mom that she already had me by my age. I'm not a child and you need to stop treating me like one. You know how hard I've worked to move forward, and part of moving forward is being able to date. To have a relationship. And I found a man who makes me feel things that—"

He raises a hand to stop me. "Please. Spare me the details."

"All I was going to say is that it's important that I be able to feel. Love. Happiness. Joy. Contentment. A connection with someone else. For so long I wasn't sure I could, but now I know that I can, and it's wonderful and I won't give it up."

"Does it have to be a Bridger?" he counters, his voice full of crankiness.

I push on. "Yes. It has to be Austin Bridger."

"Do you really see a future with him?"

Do I?

Absolutely.

I just don't know what *he's* feeling. But he did come home from Seattle for me. He did leave his mother because I needed him. My God, what a day this has been.

"I'd like to think so. But does it matter whether there's a future? He makes me feel things *now*. He makes me love my body again, Daddy." It's not something I ever expected to tell my father, but I'm not a kid and he's being ridiculously hardheaded. "He makes me want something more than to merely exist. Isn't that what *you* want for me?"

He doesn't reply right away, and I understand. What he wants mostly is my safety. He's scared to death of losing me again, and I don't blame him. But being in a protective bubble because something *might* happen isn't a life.

"You're not going to lose me," I preempt him. "Especially not to Austin Bridger."

"Carly—"

"You'll always be my father, and I'll always want you in my life. No matter who I end up with."

"You don't need anyone, Carly. You can stay here with your mother and me."

"Austin Bridger aside, you know I can't do that."

He sighs. "I know. I just didn't think you'd be ready to leave us so soon."

"I didn't say I was leaving you. I came back, didn't I? It was Austin who drove me here. He doesn't want to get between us."

"Then he shouldn't have—"

"He hasn't done anything, Daddy, except make me feel special. And important. And enough." When he stays silent, I prod, "Is it Austin Bridger you have a problem with? Or is it any man who might find me appealing?"

"I don't like the Bridgers," he says gruffly.

"You've made that more than clear," I remind him. "And I'll tell you again. You don't *know* the Bridgers. Not these Bridgers. Please give them a chance. For me."

He runs his fingers through his hair, and then he rubs his jawline. "I can't do this right now, Carly."

"But I came home."

He nods. "I know you did. And I appreciate that more than you know, but let me sleep on this. I need to get my head on straight. It's been a harrowing day for everyone. As mayor, I have to figure out what to tell the town about the dead body."

I can only nod, because he's right about that. As for the rest, it's a start, although I have a feeling I have a long way to go to convince my father of anything.

 USTIN

"SHE'LL COME BACK TO YOU," Miles says, when I return.

I don't meet his gaze as I drop the keys on a side table that looks like a slab of wood. "I'm not in the mood to talk about it right now."

He's in the great room and a ballgame is on the flatscreen TV mounted on the wall in a nook beside the massive fireplace. Whoever the interior designer was on the place did an amazing job. It makes my mom's house look so... average.

Will I ever get used to what billions can afford?

"Are you in the mood to drink about it instead?"

Chance holds up a beer bottle from his position on a leather couch. His boots are off and his sock-covered feet are up on an ottoman that also serves as an oversized coffee table.

"Brother," I say, "you're going to have to give me something a lot stronger than that."

I'm tired. Dealing with Sea-Air, and then my mom in the ER, and then flying home in a hustle because of a dead body? That's plenty. Then Carly being in the middle of that *and* dealing with her asshole father? Yeah, I'm thrilled she chose me, but fuck, if I want to be with Carly, I need to get her old man to like me. I have no idea how to do that other than to change my name and walk away from the money I've inherited. The money I need to either build the seaplane business back up or start it from scratch *and* ensure Mom has the best treatments money can buy.

"You got it." Chance rises, goes to the fancy-ass bar, and pulls a bottle of what appears to be scotch from the shelf.

"What the hell is that?"

He turns and holds up the golden liquid. "This, Austin, is twenty-five-year Macallan, aged in sherry oak casks."

I squint at it, trying to figure out what makes it special.

For me, a beer import is fancy. "I'm supposed to know what the hell that is?"

"I know what the hell that is." Miles perks up from his slouched position. "I've only had the eighteen-year, and it's sweeter than mother's milk."

"I've always been content with beer. Never had scotch," I admit. "What the hell? I'll try anything once."

Chance pours a couple fingers of the scotch for each of us in short glasses from the cabinet. He brings them to us and we clumsily clink glasses.

"What are we drinking to?" I ask.

"To you." Chance says. "To Carly."

I'm surprised, but I let it go. "Okay. I'll drink to that."

"And to Jonathan Bridger, the no-good bastard," Miles adds. "But at least he had high quality sperm, as evidenced by the fine specimens we are."

Despite my melancholy at missing Carly, that gets a laugh out of me. I raise my glass again. "To our sperm donor."

We clink again, and I take a drink of the scotch.

And oh. My. God.

It sits on my tongue for a few seconds, meandering over every taste bud and nearly giving me chills. It's smoky, woodsy, earthy, with a touch of caramel sweetness. As it slides down my throat, it doesn't catch at all. It's smooth as silk, and it leaves a subtle warmth, as if my throat is coated in the finest cashmere.

"What do you think of your first taste of scotch?" Miles nods to me.

"I think," I say, "that if being fathered by Jonathan Bridger means I can drink this stuff? Dealing with his bullshit may be worth it. Fuck, that's good."

"I've got to say"—Miles pauses as he takes another sip —"I didn't think I'd be able to tell the difference between this and the eighteen-year. But I'll be damned. The fruity oak is phenomenal."

"That's the sherry cask," Chance agrees. "Like Austin, I'm mostly a beer man, but my father did know his liquor. Not that he ever let me drink his stuff."

A haunted look passes over his face. Must be a story there, probably about how much of a dick the guy was.

"But hell, it's ours now." Chance raises his glass.

I give myself a moment to enjoy my brothers' company. These two, who I didn't want to have anything to do with mere weeks ago, have now become almost as essential to me as Carly and my mom. They went to Seattle with me. Sure, by force because of the strict rules of the will, but Chance told off the Sea-Air fucker and Miles charmed my mom.

Speaking of Carly...

"I need to check in with my girl. I promised I'd call

tonight. Then I need to check on my mom. Would you guys excuse me?"

"Absolutely." Miles raises his glass once more. "Tell them both I said hi."

"Yeah, me too," From Chance.

"Will do."

Taking my glass with me, I head into the kitchen for a bit of privacy and make the call.

"Hello?" Carly says in my ear.

"Hey, baby. You okay?" It's only been an hour since I dropped her off, but hell, I need to know. Did her dad say something since to make her feel bad? Has she changed her mind about being with me? Has she—

She sighs audibly. "It's not every day you find a dead body at work, for sure. But honestly? I think I'm doing okay."

Her voice, though slightly shaky, radiates honesty. God knows she's been through worse. "I'm glad. Everything going all right at home?"

"As well as can be expected. Dad and I have a date to talk at breakfast."

"Another breakfast, huh?"

"Right. And I won't miss this one, because I won't be in your bed."

"We can remedy that, you know. I'm really good at sneaking in. Got a trellis I can climb?"

She laughs through the phone, and it is such a joyful sound.

"As much as I'd like that, Austin, I think it might defeat the purpose of what I'm trying to do here."

I want her father to like me, not kill me with a shotgun. "I know. But I sure miss you."

"I miss you, too. But we'll see each other at lunch tomorrow."

"I'm glad everything's going okay."

"I wouldn't exactly say okay, but it's going to be fine. Eventually. What about you?"

"What about me?" I ask.

"Your mom got hurt. And that dead body? It's on your land."

She does have a point. I raise my glass and breathe in the heady fumes. "I am having twenty-five-year-old scotch with my brothers. They say hi, by the way."

"Tell them hi back. Do you like it? The scotch?"

"It's damned good." I smile into the phone. "I'm pretty sure the only thing tastier is that heaven you've got between your legs."

She's silent for a moment.

I can almost see her blushing through the phone line.

"Have I truly rendered you speechless?" I finally ask.

"I wasn't sure I could miss you more, but now all I can think about is... your tongue. *There*." Her last words are whispered so it feels like we're in a bubble of intimacy. Just the two of us.

I adjust my groin. "Damn, baby."

"Maybe tomorrow we can...you know? During lunch?"

"Abso-fucking-lutely." I'd be happy to *you know* during her lunch break.

"Wonderful. I should go. I have to get up early and have breakfast with my father at six, and I'm not missing it this time."

"I understand. I'll see you tomorrow. And Carly?"

"Yeah?"

"I can't wait."

ARLY

I JERK out of my sleep—which was a nightmare, but not about my time on the island.

No. This one was about those sightless gray eyes staring at me yesterday morning. Remembering how it felt to trip over the body. Hard, but soft, too. A person, but...not.

I blink and take a moment to adjust to the darkness. Where I am. My bed. The familiar strip of light that comes in beneath my bedroom door. The scent of pine cleaner mom uses on the wood floors. Everything is familiar. I only spent one night with Austin and I want that again. I want to be in his bed with him. Not in my sleep shirt in my twin bed with sheets my mom and I picked out on a trip to Missoula when I was in eleventh grade.

My phone is ringing. That's what woke me from my bad dream.

I fumble around, knocking it off my nightstand. I move to retrieve it, and I don't recognize the number.

"Hello?" I say breathlessly when I answer.

"Is this Carly?"

I rub my tongue over my teeth. "Yes, speaking. Who is this?"

"This is Abe Hawkins over at Bridger Ranch. I tried to get Lexie Davis on the phone, but she's not picking up. I don't know who else to call."

I wipe sleep out of my eyes. "What's wrong?"

"It's that foal she operated on. The inguinal hernia? The poor thing's running a fever, and the incision doesn't look good."

"Oh no." I'm suddenly wide awake. "Sounds like there's an infection. But I'm not a vet, Abe. I can't help you."

"You're on the list as the first person to call after Lexie and Blaine. And Blaine's still out of town."

"There are other vet techs," I say.

"Lexie put you on the list above them. Said you've had some vet school?"

She did? She listed me third? Even with my background and— he's waiting on an answer. "I have, but it was a long time ago."

Abe sighs. "Please. I don't know what to do for this poor thing. He's the offspring of one of the Bridgers' prized studs. He has to be okay."

A yawn splits my face. "All right. I'll be there soon as I can."

I stumble out of bed and throw on a pair of jeans and a long-sleeved shirt. Once my cowboy boots are on my feet, I give Ernie some loves, although he barely lifts his head from his bed in the corner, and then sneak through the house quietly so I don't wake Mom and Dad. Once I'm out of the house, I drive to the ranch. Rain is falling lightly as I park and head to the stable where the foal is recuperating from his surgery.

Abe and another hand are tending to him.

"Carly, thank God," Abe says when I walk into the stable. "The poor thing's not looking good."

The colt is lying on his side. First thing I do is check his surroundings. Everything looks clean. The hands have done a good job keeping the animal in a sterile environment.

I kneel down. "Let me take a look."

Abe's already removed the bandage and I can easily see Lexi's stitches are even and impressive, but the skin around the surgical site is raised and red, and a few streaks of pink radiate from the area outward. For a moment, I'm thankful that the horse has pink skin. If it were dark, I wouldn't be able to see this redness, which indicates the situation is serious. For a moment, I remember Ivory, the beautiful cremello mare I groomed on my first day at Bridger Ranch. Is this foal related to her? She didn't appear to have foaled recently. But this young horse has skin like hers, though his eyes are light brown and his coat a gorgeous roan.

He's in distress, and he's breathing rapidly. I don't need to recheck to see that he's feverish.

"This colt needs to survive," Abe says again. He's in his late forties and looks exhausted. We usually wear a Bridger Ranch shirt as a pseudo-uniform, but now he's sloppy in jeans and a misbuttoned shirt. The other hand doesn't look much better.

I can relate.

"Does he have a name?" I ask.

"No. Not yet."

Such a lovely animal should have a name. In my mind, I call him Beau, because he's so beautiful.

"Like you suspected, it's an infection," I tell Abe, "but I'm not a veterinarian. I can't administer medication."

"You have to do something."

"Let me get some saline. I can wash out the wound

and apply some antiseptic. Lexie's sutures are holding and they look good."

"I tried Lexie again," the other hand says. "She's still not answering."

I furrow my brow. "That doesn't sound like her. I hope she's okay."

He shakes his head.

She spent most of the day with me dealing with the dead body and then the questioning sheriff. Maybe she turned her phone off to get a good night's sleep. Maybe she went back to the bar and found that cute cowboy for a little fun. I don't have time to dwell on where my boss might be. I have a colt to help.

I rise. "I'll be right back."

I head to the vet's office located in the next stable and I grab some saline, some antiseptic and gauze. On the bookshelf sit several books about treating equines. I wish I had the time to leaf through them, but the internet is quicker. I sit at Lexie's desk and do a quick search.

Sulfadiazine seems to be the antibiotic of choice for equine infection. It's given orally, which means I'll have to shove a syringe down the poor thing's throat. Side effects are rare. Does Lexie even have any here? The next entry mentions Gentamicin, but it's generally given intra-venously, and while I've watched others do it, I've never started an IV. Procaine penicillin is another option and is given as a shot, but it can cause an anaphylactic reaction and even death in rare cases. Yeah. No thanks.

I check the shelves and the refrigerator to see what Lexie has to work with. I may not be qualified to give medicines to animals, but I don't have much choice now. It's giving antibiotics, not the actual hernia surgery.

Thank God!

She has sulfadiazine. I check Beau's chart for dosage, grab some anti-inflammatories for the fever as well, and then I hurry back to the stable.

Time is paramount, so I begin with the antibiotic and anti-inflammatory. I draw in a deep breath before administering the medication.

Trust yourself, Carly. You have to do this. If it doesn't help, at least you did something.

After giving Beau the meds, I clean the wound with the saline and antiseptic.

"Now what?" Abe asks, looking to me.

"Now, we wait. His fever should go down, and if the antibiotics are working, we should see some improvement at the incision site in a few hours." I grab my phone to check the time. "It's two a.m. I guess we're spending the night here, guys."

They settle onto the hay and lean against the stall wall.

As I clean up, a clap of thunder sounds overhead. I look up, even though I can't see through the stable's roof.

Here comes a storm. Another one for the season. It might be too much water, but it's better than a drought. I have time to think about the correlation to my life. It's either crazy and insane or nothing. I have all the feels or none.

I have to decide which is best.

No, I don't need time to decide. I know.

————

"CARLY?" Someone shakes my shoulder.

I open my eyes. Blink. Rain is drumming on the roof of the stable. I'm surprised it didn't wake me up, but then I've had a day. And a night. It's the second time I've been woken up tonight.

"I didn't mean to fall asleep."

My eyes adjust. It's Lexie. She's soaking wet from the rain.

"I'm so sorry, Carly. You too, Abe. Jim. I must've forgotten to plug my phone in last night, and it died. I don't know what's the matter with me. I'm just so... that body yesterday... but that's no excuse. When I woke up a few minutes ago and plugged the phone in, I saw your message. How is he doing?"

"Carly's been helpful," Abe says. "Look, he's doing better."

Lexie turns and examines Beau, taking his temperature once again, and then checking the incision site. "His fever is down. The site is infected, like you all thought. What did you give him, Carly?"

I push to my feet, brushing straw from my bottom. I rattle off the medication and dosage in a robotic tone, hoping I haven't done more harm than good.

Lexie smiles as she places the earpieces of her stethoscope in her ears. "Nice job. I might've given a little less of the sulfadiazine, but there's no harm in the dose you gave him. You may have saved his life."

"Thank God." I sigh. "Abe says he's the offspring of a prize horse, and I thought... If I didn't do something..."

"You did everything right," she assures me. "I'm the one to blame here. I shouldn't have been so careless about my phone. It might be worth getting my landline reinstalled. Especially on a night like we had tonight. The cell towers may go down."

At the mention of her phone, I look at mine. Five thirty a.m. I scramble to my feet. "If it's okay, I have to go. I'm supposed to have breakfast with my father at six."

"You should call him," Lexie says. "Explain what's happened here. I don't think you're going to make it. That storm is nasty. They expect flash flooding. There are warnings all over the news."

"I'll make it. I grew up here, remember? I've driven through storms like this. It's really important that I not miss this breakfast date with my dad."

She eyes me but doesn't push. "All right, but please be careful. Don't worry about coming into work this morning. Try to get some sleep after breakfast."

"Thank you. I appreciate that."

"No, thank *you*. You, Abe and Jim saved this little guy's life. I should've been here, and I wasn't." She smiles at me again. "I'd hate to lose you around here, Carly, but you need to go back to vet school. You have great instinct, and you love animals. You need to be treating them."

"I'd like to," I say. "But I'm taking life one step at a time these days, and the step I need to take right now is breakfast with my father. I'll be in later."

She shakes her head. "Nonsense. Take the day off. If I see you in here today, you're fired." She places the diaphragm of her stethoscope against Beau's chest.

I glance at Abe, who gives me a shooing motion. Jim just gives me a small smile. "All right. I'll take you up on it, but only this time." I turn and leave the stables.

The rain is pummeling down, and the ground is soft and muddy. Lexie wasn't kidding.

Again I'm surprised the noise of the storm didn't wake

me up before Lexie got there, but I learned to blank out noxious screaming and grunting noises during those years I spent in captivity.

I get into my car and begin the drive home. If I hurry, I should just make it.

I've got my wipers going as fast they'll go, but visibility is non-existent. Good thing no one's on the road this early. Ranchers get up before dawn, but they're not going anywhere besides their barn or stables to do chores. They're taking care of animals.

The county road isn't bad at first, but as I near the bridge over the creek...

Damn. This isn't just any flash flood. Usually the flooding happens after the rain starts to subside, especially if the storm is upstream. Right now? It's coming down like a firestorm and the creek has risen over the bridge. There's no way I'll get across.

I know the rules of a flash flood. Don't try to drive through it. Leave the car and get to high ground.

I'll have to call my father after all and let him know that I won't make breakfast. That I'm actually not in my bed. If he finds me gone, I don't know what he'll think. No, I know *exactly* what he'll think and it won't be good. He'll panic. Think I ditched him in a disrespectful way for Austin.

I should've left a note but I didn't even think of it.

I grab my phone, but the rising waters are coming toward the car. I try to reverse, but I feel the car start to lift. Shit, I have to move. I escape the car before calling him.

"Oh!" I cry out, the sound ripped away by the wind and heavy rain.

I hit the ground with a thud. The slick mud made me lose my footing and I fall flat on my face. My phone slips from my grasp, and lands...

I have no idea where. It's quickly washed away. I pull myself up, ignoring the pain on my palms, which are scratched up from trying to break my fall. Great, a lovely mixture of mud and blood. I glance down at my feet, the cold water already filling my shoes and swirling around my ankles.

That's the last thought I give to my father or to breakfast. I glance at my car. The water has already buried my tires by a few inches.

Wet and muddy, my heart doing flips, I trudge away from the swiftly swelling creek along the road toward higher ground. I'm soaked through to the skin and I need to get to safety. A broken tree branch is caught on the muddy torrent and whacks me in the shin. I'm no match for water. Nothing is.

I didn't survive years in captivity to die this way.

I have to move. And fast.

 USTIN

You've got to be kidding me.

Someone's pounding on my freaking bedroom door. Again.

I'm already up, just coming out of the bathroom. Chance has Miles and me trained now, but damn. I blearily glance across the room to the clock on the side table. It's barely six.

"What the fuck do you want?" I yell.

"You decent?"

Of course. Chance's voice.

I'm in my boxers. "Barely."

The door opens, and Chance walks in.

"Sure, please come in." I roll my eyes.

"Hey, is Carly here? Please tell me she's here."

A jolt of fear lances through me. I stiffen and narrow my gaze. "No. She went home last night. You know that. I took her myself."

"I know, but her father's on the phone. Apparently they were supposed to have breakfast this morning, and she's not there."

"What?" That lance of fear morphs into all-out panic. "What do you mean she's not there?" I shout.

"Talk to him yourself." He holds out his cell.

I grab it from him and put it to my ear. "Mr. Vance?"

"Where the hell is she, Bridger?"

"She's not here. I swear to God. I dropped her off last night. I watched her go inside, even spoke with your wife."

"That's correct," he replies.

"No note?" I ask.

"No."

Chance is watching me, easily following the conversation.

"We need to find her. Where could she have gone, and why?"

"Stop lying to me, Bridger," he snaps.

I run a hand through my hair. "Mayor, this is serious. I don't know where she is. You have a right to be panicked. I am, too. Please. We need to work together to figure this out. What can you tell me? Was her bed slept in?"

Silence for a few seconds, until—

"Yes. Her bed is unmade."

"Oh fuck. *Fuck*. You don't think..." I don't want to say the rest, that someone may have taken her from her bed.

"You think I wouldn't have heard if someone came into my house and took my daughter?"

"I don't know. I just don't know." I run my fingers through my hair again, scratch my forehead, nearly breaking skin. "We've got to find her. Where are you? Still at the house?"

"Yeah. The rain is finally starting to die down."

"Why don't I—"

Miles runs into my room. He's got on jeans and a shirt, still unbuttoned. His feet are bare and he's wet, clearly having been out in the rain. "Hey, I've got some news."

"Hold on a minute, Mayor. I'm going to put you on speakerphone. Miles says he knows something."

"Hey, Mayor," Miles says. "Can you hear me?"

"Yeah," comes Vance's voice to the phone.

"I talked to Lexie at the stables. That's Dr. Davis, our vet. Apparently Carly got a call from one of the hands in the middle of the night to come look at a colt that just had surgery. They called her because they couldn't get hold of Lexie."

"So she's there then, at the ranch?" Vance says, his voice full of worry.

I feel a hint of hope that she's okay.

Miles glances my way. "No. Lexie says she left around five-thirty, said she had a breakfast date with you."

"She's not back yet," he replies.

"All right." Chance's voice remains steady. "Then we know she's somewhere between here and your place, Mayor."

"The storm," I say. "You don't think..."

"Carly grew up here," Vance says. "She's seen storms like this."

"I've never seen a storm like this," Chance offers. "I grew up here as well. Austin, let's go. We'll get in the four-by-four and find her."

"I'll start the other way," Vance says.

"All right." Chance rubs his unshaven jaw. "Whoever finds her first, call the other right away with the location."

"You got it." Vance ends the call on his end.

My body has gone numb. Completely numb. My fingers lose their feeling, and Chance's phone clatters onto the hardwood floor at my bare feet.

He picks it up. "Hey. We're going to find her. Carly's a smart girl. Resourceful. And she knows how to help herself."

I don't reply.

I don't doubt any of my brother's words. I have full faith in Carly to take care of herself.

My faith, however, stops when others are involved. What if someone blindsided her and she ran off the road? What if she's lying somewhere in a ditch? Unable to help herself?

Or worse...

I can't go there.

I absolutely cannot lose Carly.

Because...

Fuck.

I love her.

I fucking love her.

And we didn't know where she was, in a storm. Alone.

"Austin." Miles snaps me out of my thoughts. "We have to go. Now."

I'm still in my boxers.

"Get some clothes on," Chance says. "As soon as you're ready, we're out of here."

———

No.

This can't be Carly's car.

The vehicle is off the road, and it looks like it slid a dozen feet or more to the side. A mud slick, at least six inches thick, coats the pavement. It's clear the creek flooded the banks with not just water, but debris and dirt from upstream. The bridge didn't wash out, but it's a fucking mess.

"Austin..." Miles's voice. "From the debris line on the side of her car, it doesn't look like it was hit too bad. The mayor hasn't gotten here yet. She was clearly closer to our place."

"I'll call the mayor."

As soon as Chance brings the truck to a stop, I bolt. It's barely raining now but the sky is thick and heavy with clouds and possibly more rain. The wind's strong, but I don't even feel it.

I run to the car.

"Carly!"

I pull on the door handle, but it's locked, and she's not in the driver seat. I pound on the window. "Carly! Carly! Carly!"

I'm shouting at nothing because she's not inside. I'm not sure if that's a good or bad thing.

Meanwhile, my brothers walk around the vehicle.

"Good," Chance says from the back. He must've made the call with the mayor a short one. "Clearly, she wasn't in a collision. The car is fine."

"Fine!" I grit out and wave my arms. "What about this is fine? She's not here. Someone... Someone took her.

Someone fucking took her again!" I grab the sides of my hair and pull. "Fuck!"

Chance inches toward me. "Austin. No. What are the chances of—"

"The chances are good! They took her once, and they want her again! Damn it!"

Miles ambles toward us, and—

Crack.

"What was that?" He leans down. "Oh."

"What is it?" Chance asks.

"A phone. A cracked phone now."

"Let me see."

He hands it to me.

I recognize it instantly. "It's Carly's. This is her case, with a golden retriever on it. Her phone. They made her give up her phone!" I throw the phone back on the wet ground, lean against the wet car, and bang my head on the roof as the rain continues to pelt me.

"Hey," Miles says. "Here comes the mayor."

"Yeah, he said he was almost here," Chance replies.

I don't care. He can blame me if he wants. Because I don't care. If Carly is gone...

Fuck!

The oncoming car screeches to a halt, dredging up water and splashing the three of us.

I don't care.

I don't care about any of this.

"Where is she?" Vance demands as he exits his vehicle.

"There's no evidence of a collision," Chance says. "She's not here, Mayor."

"Damn it!"

I hear him stomp his feet on the wet road.

I don't move.

"Damn it all, Bridger," he says, although I'm not sure who he's talking to. Until he gets in my face.

"Hey"—Chance's voice—"you leave my brother alone. Can't you see this is killing him?"

"Killing *him*?" Vance snarls. "What do you think it's doing to Darla and me? We already lost her once."

I don't bother moving my head. I don't bother facing Mayor Vance.

I don't bother doing anything, because I have no will left.

I came back from Seattle for Carly. I chose her.

And now...

She's gone. My Carly is gone.

"Let's call the sheriff," Chance says. "Get a search party started."

"Search party?" Vance says. "No search party will find her. They couldn't find her the last time."

"Mayor, listen to reason," Miles says. "It was a bad

storm. She may have just left her car when the water—Wait. What the hell is that?"

"Oh my God," Mayor Vance gasps. "Carly? Carly, are you all right?"

Carly?

Finally, I move, and I look toward their voices.

And I see an angel.

An angel coming down from the hillside the creek was carved from, the rain, a hazy fog around her.

"Carly!" Vance shouts.

I don't say a word. I run. I race toward her, nearly slipping on the wet grass, and I grab her in my arms. "Oh my God, Carly. Thank God!"

She melts into me. She's soaked through and chilled. It's a warm morning, but she's been out in the elements for a while and the wind is strong.

"What happened, baby?" I hold her tight and then pull back, hold her shoulders so I can trace over her body. Make sure she's not hurt. That she's whole.

"I'm okay," she says. "I should have never tried to make that trip. I just didn't want to miss breakfast with my dad again, you know?"

"None of it matters." I yank her close again, kissing the top of her wet head. "All that matters is that you're okay."

"Of course I'm okay," she says. "I know how to deal

with a flash flood, although this is one of the worst ones I've ever seen."

"What were you thinking?" This from her father, who has joined us. "Trying to drive in this?"

I loosen my hold. A little.

"I didn't want to miss our breakfast again, Daddy. I didn't want you to think... well, that happened anyway."

"My God." Mayor Vance rubs his forehead, droplets of water sliding down his cheeks from the action. "Carly, precious, I'm so sorry."

"It's okay." She gives him a soft smile. "I'm fine. See? I was going to call you to tell you I wasn't going to make it, but when I got out of my car, I dropped my phone. I couldn't find it because the rain was coming down so hard it was blinding me. The water rose so fast, before I knew it was ankle deep. I knew I had to get to higher ground. There was no way I could drive. I tried to back out and my car started to lift."

"Where did you go?" I ask, glancing around.

"I walked up the road a bit, back toward the ranch, and found one of the old sheds on Bridger land."

"Damn," Chance says. His Stetson has kept his face dry, but droplets fall off the brim and wet the shoulders of his shirt. "One of the tasks on my list was to get rid of all those old structures that we don't use anymore. Now we'll get them stocked for emergencies instead."

"I'm glad it was there," Carly says. "I was able to get out of the rain and wait it out. I didn't mean to worry anyone."

I kiss the top of her wet head again. "I know that. We all do. Right, Mayor?"

He nods, which is the first time he and I agree on anything.

"My God," I breathe. "Nothing else matters now. You're here, and you're safe."

She pulls away then and I let her. Barely. Goes to her father and hugs him. "I'm sorry, Daddy."

"You don't have to be sorry." Vance tips his daughter's chin up so she looks at him. "I'm the one who's sorry. I'm sorry I've been so..." He shakes his head.

"It's all right, Daddy. I understand. You and Mom are just scared. Scared of losing me again. But I promise you that I'm not going anywhere."

"He's leaving, only here for the will," he tells her.

I stiffen at the implication, but he's right. *Was* right. "I'm not leaving Carly. Who knows what a year will bring? She might leave me for vet school. But I'll follow her anywhere. Hell, I'll even stay here with my pain-in-the-ass brothers if that's what Carly wants."

"I want to be with Austin." She glances at me. Love shines in her eyes.

My heart nearly bursts. Love for this woman flows through me, and the intensity of it astounds me.

I want to confess my love to her, but right here? In front of my brothers? In front of her father?

Carly steps away from her father then.

I take my chance to grab her.

"Don't you ever do that to me again, Carly Vance. Don't you ever leave me again."

She sinks her head into my chest. "I don't want to, Austin. Not ever."

"Good. Because I love you. I love you so damned much."

Yeah, I didn't wait. Because I've learned that I have to live in the here and now. Grasp happiness where I can. And I'm going to find it with this woman. She and I. Together.

 ARLY

AUSTIN'S WORDS PERMEATE ME. Infuse me with warmth. Though I'm soaking wet, dirty with mud, and a complete mess, none of that matters.

I feel like the most beautiful princess in the world nestled in Austin's arms, his words of love flowing around us and protecting us like a soft cloud.

"I love you, too," I say against him. "So much."

We stay in our cloud for a moment, just the two of us.

Until a throat clears.

It's my father. Yeah, maybe not the best time to profess our love for each other. My cheeks heat.

I pull away. "Daddy?"

He clears his throat. "I owe you an apology, Bridger. All of you, actually."

"It's all right, Mayor." Chance sets his thumbs in the front pocket of his jeans.

I look up at Austin, and all I see in his face is pure relief. Pure happiness that I'm here.

My father steps forward. "You seem to truly care about my daughter."

"I do, Mayor. It wasn't my intention to profess my love to her in front of you and my brothers, but when I was faced with losing her..."

"You both need to chill," Carly says. "Neither of you is *ever* going to lose me. I know how to take care of myself."

"You do, sweetheart," Dad says. "I'm sorry I didn't have more faith in you."

"It's okay. I understand."

"You'd *better* not be going anywhere," Austin adds.

My father sticks his hand out then, and Austin shakes it. He moves on to Chance and Miles next.

It's a start. My father will never love the Bridgers. He'll always associate them with their father and whatever bad things he did. But he's willing to try.

That's all I ask for. Because I never want to have to pick. I just learned my heart is big enough for the man who raised me and the man I want to spend my life with.

"You need to get out of the weather. Some dry clothes," Dad advises.

We're all waterlogged, but I'm muddy and there's grass in my hair.

I don't disagree, but he surprises me with his next words.

"Go with Austin, sweetheart. He'll take care of you."

I feel Austin's fingers lightly squeeze my hip. Yeah, he's stunned too.

"Daddy?"

"Go. Be happy. And be home for dinner."

He's actually smiling, which makes me smile.

"Six o'clock, Austin. I'm sure you'll like my wife's pot roast."

He's inviting Austin?

"Yes, sir. I'm sure I will."

I feel like a fish with my mouth opening and closing, but he turns and heads to his truck before I can say anything.

We watch in silence as he drives off.

Miles heads to my car, opens the door and drops into the seat. He grunts because his knees don't fit under the steering wheel. Reaching down, he uses the lever and pushes the seat back. "If there isn't any hydrolock, this should start right up. Good thing it's an older model and not electronic based."

He tries the ignition and it does start. Miles looks to me and winks.

"Don't worry, sweetheart. A little detailing and it'll be as good as new," he calls. "Although if you let me spend a little time with this baby, I'll have it all tricked out."

Chance tosses Austin the keys to his big truck.

"I'll ride with Miles...if I can fit." He gives me a smile and a wink and then folds himself into my passenger seat.

Miles does a U-turn and heads back to the ranch.

"Do they remind you of two clowns in a circus car?" Austin asks as he pulls me into his side.

We're left alone in the middle of the road along with the roar of the swollen creek.

Austin pulls me close. Holds me tightly, almost too tightly, but I don't care.

We're soggy and he's remarkably warm and perfect. He kisses the top of my head.

"Woman, you scared ten years off my life. Fuck."

"I'm sorry. I—"

"Don't be sorry. You didn't do anything wrong. Except leave my side. I think the best thing is to never let you out of my sight. Or my hold."

I nuzzle his damp shirt. "I think that's a good idea."

"Your dad doesn't hate me."

There is a mixture of surprise and wonder in his voice, the same that I feel.

"I know. I think we should celebrate."

"I'm game. How?" he asks.

"A shower," I reply. With his body heat warming my front, the rest of me is starting to chill.

Austin laughs and I feel it through our joined chests.

"Perfect idea."

"Especially since I'm not to leave your hold."

He pushes me back just enough so he can lean down. Our eyes meet. "Got something in mind?"

I smile. "So many things."

"Will we have enough hot water for all of them?"

USTIN

THIRTY MINUTES LATER, our wet clothes are a soggy pile on my bathroom floor. Steam billows from the hot water. I've got my hands in Carly's long hair, working the shampoo into a thick lather.

I have her where I want her. With me and safe. I see every inch of her, know she's not hurt, doesn't even have a bruise—only the scars, the scars that make her who she is. The dirt and tiny pebbles that clung to her clothes and body washed down the drain.

My dick is long and hard and aches to be in her, but it's not his turn. I need to tend to my woman.

Then I'll sink into her and make sure she knows she's mine.

"Did you hear more about your mom?" she asks.

If there's one sentence that stalls my need to claim her, it's that one. Talking about my mother and the fact that she fell. And that I'm not there with her.

I still feel torn, pulled between those I love.

Carly's whole and safe, and the dead body can't get any deader.

"The surgery was successful. Usually, it's an outpatient procedure, which is a little insane, but she'll spend the night and then go to rehab."

She turns in my arms and I tip her head back beneath the spray. Her eyes are closed as I rinse the suds.

"You want to be there."

I look down at her, the water droplets sliding down her cheeks. Her full mouth. I can't resist. I kiss her gently and then finish rinsing the last of the shampoo from her hair.

"I do. But when you meet her, you'll understand. She's stubborn. Muleheaded. She doesn't want someone looming over her or being coddled."

She reaches up, wipes her hair, and then turns from the spray. "Sounds familiar."

"Mmm," I say, looking over every inch of her perfection.

"You can go back," she prompts.

"With Miles and Chance in tow. And you, because I'm not leaving you behind to get into any other mischief."

She sputters and then laughs. "Then maybe she can come here. Visit or stay awhile. You said she can't be a pilot any longer."

I can't help but smile at her thoughtful spirit. "I'm sure she'll like the idea, but even if she's grounded, she won't want to leave the business for long. She's a real taskmaster."

Carly reaches up and cups my neck with her hand. "I can't wait to meet her."

Mom will love Carly, no question. Her idea's a good one, having Mom come here to the ranch.

"I'll bring up the idea with her. Later."

My hands begin to roam, and I reach to shut off the water.

I snag Carly's hand and pull her from the shower. I don't waste time drying either of us off and tug her all the way to my bed.

Our bed.

I toss her on it and she bounces with a laugh.

I settle on top of her, straddling her hips and my hands beside her head.

"You okay?" I ask. She hasn't shown any signs of being afraid of me, but I always pause to check.

She bites her lip, nods, reaches up and grasps me. Her small hand doesn't even wrap all the way around the base of my dick.

I hiss at the sweet contact.

"You okay?" she asks back.

"Baby, I'm more than okay," I tell her. "I'm going to kiss every inch of your body before I sink into you."

"Promises, promises," she says on a grin.

The once shy Carly is replaced with a playful one. She's confident and brazen.

"You want promises, baby? How about this? I love you. We're in this together. Whatever *this* is, it's you and me."

She nods. "You and me."

"Be a good girl and tell me where you want me to kiss you first."

Her green eyes darken and she taps her lip with a finger.

Her mouth? I'll happily start there.

But it moves, that finger, down the center line of her body. Between her breasts and lower to her navel. Lower still to her parted thighs. I see the scars and know that the woman beneath me is so strong. So brave.

Perfect.

"Here," she whispers.

Yeah, fucking perfect, I think, and then I lower my head.

EPILOGUE

$\mathcal{M}$ILES

"DECIDE TO COME UP FOR AIR?" I smile when Austin and Carly finally grace us with their presence at the dinner table.

Carly's cheeks are flushed pink, and Austin's hair is a tousled mass of brown. Yeah, they both look *just fucked*. Make that *just fucked on steroids*. They've been in Austin's room since he and Carly came back this morning.

"Actually, I was sleeping." Carly blushes further.

Right.

"You don't owe them any explanation." Austin gives her a pussy-whipped smile.

"As you know," she continues, "I didn't get any sleep last night because I was tending to your colt."

"Which we appreciate." Chance reaches for the platter in the middle of the table. The dishes are set out family style in brown clay serving platters. Salsa, chopped onion and cilantro, seasoned rice, and black beans. "I didn't see either of you come out for lunch so I assume you're starving. Louisa made chicken flautas."

"Who? Your cook?" Carly settles in with Chance on one side, Austin on the other.

I'm across from her.

"The housekeeper," Chance corrects. "She keeps this entire place running."

I introduced myself when she placed my clean laundry on my bed. I'm not used to anyone taking care of me. It's so different from New York, where no one knows anyone. We just call each other "hey" or "you."

"Looks great." Austin takes the platter from Chance. "I love Mexican food."

"Yeah. Me too. The spicier the better." The robust scent of chiles has my mouth watering. I grab my cold Mexican beer, squeeze the lime wedge into the bottle, and take a long drink. Good stuff.

I'm about to take the platter from Austin when the doorbell rings.

The housekeeper—Louisa—comes in a minute

later. She's in her late fifties with salt and pepper hair. She's in jeans and a green top, and a gentle smile tugs at her mouth. "It's Detective Peterson from the Bayfield sheriff's office. He wants to speak to all three of you."

Chance sets down his fork with the sigh. "In the middle of dinner?"

"Says it's important."

"I guess that's my cue." Austin rises and kisses Carly's cheek as Louisa leaves the room. "Be right back, sweetheart."

I have no choice but to follow my brothers out of the dining room and to the doorway, leaving my beer and grub behind. This isn't wholly unexpected. A dead body was just found on our property, after all. But it's dinnertime.

The detective is a few years older than we are. Solemn looking, with bloodshot gray eyes. He wears scuffed brown cowboy boots, dark denims, and a striped button down. He's armed with a handgun strapped at his waist. I don't recall seeing him as part of the crew dealing with retrieving the dead body.

"Hey, Mark," Chance says.

He knows everyone in town. In comparison to his relationship with the mayor, Chance seems neutral toward the guy.

"Chance." The man tips his head. "You two must be Austin and Miles."

Austin holds out his hand. "Austin Bridger."

"Detective Mark Peterson. I'm investigating the murder that took place on your land."

"Murder?" I cock my head and withdraw the hand Peterson hasn't yet shaken. "I didn't realize it was official."

"We're still waiting on the autopsy," Peterson says, "but we treat all dead bodies in situations like this as homicide until we can rule it out. That means the three of you— along with your deceased father—are prime suspects."

"Suspects? Now wait a damned minute." Austin closes the distance between himself and the detective. "Miles and I weren't even in the state when that guy met his maker."

"That has yet to be determined," Peterson replies.

I didn't see the body, but from what I heard from those who did, the guy was in rough shape. He'd been there a while, stuck beneath the deep water of the creek until we broke up the dam and it receded.

"Doesn't matter," the detective continues. "As of right now, I'm ordering the three of you not to leave town until you hear otherwise. You need to be on hand for question-ing. I hear you were in Seattle recently. Don't leave again."

Invisible insects bite at the back of my neck. Is this guy for real? "You've got a lot of nerve," I say. "We were the ones out there breaking up that dam. Would we have done that if we knew we were going to unearth a guy we murdered? If not for us, he'd still be out there."

"I've been doing this a long time." Peterson sucks at his teeth and tucks a thumb into his belt. "I wouldn't put anything past Jonathan Bridger's progeny. I admit, learning he has two additional sons makes my job a lot easier. All I have to do is drive to this ranch to find the criminals."

Yeah. He's making it pretty fucking clear where this is going. I'm no small-town boy. I'm from New York, and I can smell a dirty cop a mile away. At least one who likes to cut corners and not follow the evidence.

"You know shit about us," I mutter, my hands curling into fists.

Peterson shrugs. "Don't have to."

I see red. The guy's already pinned this mess on us. "You fucking son of a—"

I lunge, but Chance pulls me back.

"Easy, Miles," he says by my ear. "I don't know what you're used to in New York, but you can't manhandle cops around here."

Austin steps toward the detective, blocking me from him. "My brother's right. This is insane. You know Miles and I had nothing to with this. Our only crime is that we were sired by Jonathan Bridger. And Chance? The big lug wouldn't hurt a fly."

"You sure about that?"

A vein in Chance's temple throbs, but he says nothing.

"Why the fuck would he kill someone on his own land?" I ask.

Peterson shifts his gaze from Chance to me. "You have enough of it. Lots of places to hide a body."

I break free of Chance's grasp, but instead of flying at Peterson and rearranging his face, I stomp past him and out to the garage next to the main house where my classic Harley Softail waits for me. I bought it from the classifieds in the local paper the other day. It's in rough shape, but I know a good thing when I see it. Some TLC and she'll be incredible, just like all my other projects.

If I don't get the hell out of here, I'm not sure what I'll do. So much for a beer and some delicious flautas. I can't sit at that table and pretend Peterson's not going to fuck us all over. One thing's for sure. I will *not* go down for the murder of some poor SOB who somehow washed downstream onto Bridger land.

Peterson is out for blood. Bridger blood. He's got the look, and I'm feeling that slimy sensation, like lizards are scrambling beneath my skin.

He's definitely dirty, and he wants to take down Jonathan Bridger. Unlike the mayor, where his beef was personal, this is different. Worse. Since our dad's six feet under, Peterson will settle for us instead. I've seen it in New York, but I didn't expect to encounter it in Bayfield, Montana.

I crank the engine, listen to the lusty growling of the chrome pipes, kick the bike into gear, and scream out into the evening. I thought my time in Montana was going to be easy. Simple. Boring.

Fuck, was I wrong.

***

See what happens next for Miles in Flawed, Book 2 in The Billion Heirs series. Read now!

The bad boy brother. The by-the-books detective. A random meeting that will change their lives.

Miles Bridger would rather be home in New York than stuck on a Montana ranch with his newfound half brothers, thanks to his deadbeat dad's will. Miles now works with bulls and hay bales instead of custom bikes. He keeps his sense of humor about the whole thing...until a dead body surfaces on the ranch and he and his brothers are thrown headfirst into a murder investigation.

Sadie Hopkins plays by the rules in her job as detective, so she's only too happy to turn a little naughty during a bachelorette party dare. Heat flares between Sadie and the gorgeous blond man she approaches, but when a high-profile case crosses her desk the next day, she's in for a surprise. The man from the bar is none other than Miles Bridger...and he's a murder suspect.

Despite this revelation, Miles and Sadie's chemistry sizzles. But the flawed Miles doesn't do relationships, and Sadie's past crashes into the present with a surprising discovery that could spell danger for both of them.

BONUS CONTENT

Guess what? We've got some bonus content for you with Carly and Austin. Yup, there's more!

Click here to read!

A NOTE FROM HELEN

Dear Reader,

Thank you for reading *Scarred*. If you want to find out about my current backlist and future releases, please visit my website, like my Facebook page, and join my mailing list. If you're a fan, please join my Facebook street team (Hardt & Soul) to help spread the word about my books. I regularly do awesome giveaways for my street team members.

If you enjoyed the story, please take the time to leave a review. I welcome all feedback.

I wish you all the best!

Helen

Sign up for my newsletter here:

http://www.helenhardt.com/signup

GET A FREE VANESSA VALE BOOK!

Join my mailing list to be the first to know of new releases, free books, special prices and other author giveaways.

http://freeromanceread.com

ALSO BY HELEN HARDT

Follow Me Series:

Follow Me Darkly

Follow Me Under

Follow Me Always

Darkly

Wolfes of Manhattan

Rebel

Recluse

Runaway

Rake

Reckoning

Billionaire Island (Wolfes continuation)

Escape

Gems of Wolfe Island (Wolfes continuation)

Moonstone

Raven

Sex and the Season:

Lily and the Duke

Rose in Bloom

Lady Alexandra's Lover

Sophie's Voice

Temptation Saga:

Tempting Dusty

Teasing Annie

Taking Catie

Taming Angelina

Treasuring Amber

Trusting Sydney

Tantalizing Maria

Standalone Novels and Novellas

Reunited

Misadventures:

Misadventures of a Good Wife (with Meredith Wild)

Misadventures with a Rockstar

The Cougar Chronicles:

The Cowboy and the Cougar

Calendar Boy

Daughters of the Prairie:

The Outlaw's Angel

Lessons of the Heart

Song of the Raven

Collections:

Destination Desire

Her Two Lovers

Non-Fiction:

got style?

ALSO BY VANESSA VALE

For the most up-to-date listing of my books:

vanessavalebooks.com

The Billion Heirs

Scarred

Flawed

Broken

Alpha Mountain

Hero

Rebel

Warrior

Billionaire Ranch

North

South

East

West

Bachelor Auction

Teach Me The Ropes

Hand Me The Reins

Back In The Saddle

Wolf Ranch

Rough

Wild

Feral

Savage

Fierce

Ruthless

Two Marks

Untamed

Tempted

Desired

Enticed

More Than A Cowboy

Strong & Steady

Rough & Ready

Wild Mountain Men

Mountain Darkness

Mountain Delights

Mountain Desire

Mountain Danger

Grade-A Beefcakes

Sir Loin of Beef

T-Bone

Tri-Tip

Porterhouse

Skirt Steak

Small Town Romance

Montana Fire

Montana Ice

Montana Heat

Montana Wild

Montana Mine

Steele Ranch

Spurred

Wrangled

Tangled

Hitched

Lassoed

Bridgewater County

Ride Me Dirty

Claim Me Hard

Take Me Fast

Hold Me Close

Make Me Yours

Kiss Me Crazy

Mail Order Bride of Slate Springs

A Wanton Woman

A Wild Woman

A Wicked Woman

Bridgewater Ménage

Their Runaway Bride

Their Kidnapped Bride

Their Wayward Bride

Their Captivated Bride

Their Treasured Bride

Their Christmas Bride

Their Reluctant Bride

Their Stolen Bride

Their Brazen Bride

Their Rebellious Bride

Their Reckless Bride

Bridgewater Brides World

Lenox Ranch Cowboys

Cowboys & Kisses

Spurs & Satin

Reins & Ribbons

Brands & Bows

Lassos & Lace

Montana Men

The Lawman

The Cowboy

The Outlaw

Standalones

Relentless

All Mine & Mine To Take

Bride Pact

Rough Love

Twice As Delicious

Flirting With The Law

Mistletoe Marriage

Man Candy - A Coloring Book

ABOUT HELEN HARDT

#1 *New York Times*, #1 *USA Today*, and #1 *Wall Street Journal* bestselling author Helen Hardt's passion for the written word began with the books her mother read to her at bedtime. She wrote her first story at age six and hasn't stopped since. In addition to being an award-winning author of romantic fiction, she's a mother, an attorney, a black belt in Taekwondo, a grammar geek, an appreciator of fine red wine, and a lover of Ben and Jerry's ice cream. She writes from her home in Colorado, where she lives with her family. Helen loves to hear from readers.

Please sign up for her newsletter here:
http://www.helenhardt.com/signup
Visit her here:
http://www.helenhardt.com

ABOUT VANESSA VALE

A USA Today bestseller, Vanessa Vale writes tempting romance with unapologetic bad boys who don't just fall in love, they fall hard. Her 80+ books have sold over one million copies. She lives in the American West where she's always finding inspiration for her next story. While she's not as skilled at social media as her kids, she loves to interact with readers.

vanessavaleauthor.com

facebook.com/vanessavaleauthor
twitter.com/iamvanessavale
instagram.com/vanessa_vale_author
amazon.com/Vanessa-Vale/e/B00PGB3AXC
bookbub.com/profile/vanessa-vale
tiktok.com/@vanessavaleauthor

Made in the USA
Coppell, TX
13 October 2022

84600576R00208